Another
Time for $Love$

OTHER BOOKS AND AUDIO BOOKS

BY LYNNE LARSON

In the Shadow of an Angel

Saving Lucie Cole

a novel

Another Time for Love

When two worlds collide...

Lynne Larson

Covenant Communications, Inc.

Salt Lake County—Present Day

Chapter One

WHENEVER SAM CARROLL THOUGHT OF the accident, he remembered mostly colors—the silver glint of the Dodge Viper five yards in front of him on I-15, the cherry red of his own '99 Mustang, its speeding tires barely touching the pavement, and mostly the blur of the Buick as it shot across his peripheral vision like a blue torch, squeezing into his lane behind the Dodge and scraping a large swath of paint from his left door before sliding sideways in front of him. There was a piercing squeal of brakes, and then the inevitable impact, a grinding of steel against steel, before the Buick flipped over the hood of the Mustang and landed upside down in the opposite lane, narrowly missing a Suburban, which went spinning toward the shoulder.

Sam saw none of this. The air bag exploded with the first metallic shudder and erased it all. The colors faded to black. The Viper was long gone. Soon the wail of sirens was all that Sam could hear, and even that seemed dull and far away. He was locked inside himself, alive but unable to respond, to see, to talk, to move. Barely able to hear. Pain seared through every fiber in his body. His brain was pulsating. Sometimes he could think with great clarity; the images were vivid, the lines sharp. Then in an instant everything would drain away as if his senses were being sucked down a pipe. He'd have to fight to get them back, to bring reality bubbling to the surface once again.

An oxygen mask covered his mouth and nose. He was strapped down to a gurney and shoved forward, his body rigid, his neck and head braced and immovable. He remembered freaking out, terror-stricken. He'd tried to scream. He'd tried to shriek. Where was the morphine drip? The throbbing in his head was killing him. *Please, give me something! Give me something for the pain!*

But the pleading frenzy was only in his mind. He couldn't speak. He couldn't open his mouth to cry. The urgent voices of the paramedics were all he knew. The gurney wheels bumping across the pavement and the motion of the lift sliding him through the doors of the ambulance were all he felt. Then had come the jerk of acceleration and the squeal of the siren once again, and Sam was left to wonder in utter confusion who would move his beautiful red Mustang off the road.

Funny, how life can change so suddenly, Sam mused during a lucid moment. One minute you're flying down I-15 in your mint-condition '99 Mustang, without a care in the world. The sprawling city—your city— before you, with its familiar streets and neighborhoods, its homes nestled on the ridges, its soaring peaks standing sentinel in the east. Your home, your Zion. All is well. The next minute you're lying on the asphalt at Point of the Mountain, smoke coming out of your ears and your scalp on fire. Urgent voices barking orders. Strong hands lifting your dead weight. Not what a young guy expects after five years of dashing helter-skelter through a joyful bachelorhood dedicated to hot cars, cool clothes, and beautiful women—lots of beautiful women, coeds and professional types from Pocatello to Provo. He'd had the world by the tail, and now this. Lights glared down at him in the emergency room. His eyes were sensitive to light, but he couldn't make out any objects. At least not well enough to know he wasn't blind. Light and shadow, that's all he saw. Voices and movement he could follow; light and shadow moved in and out, back and forth. They were laboring over him, attaching tubes and needles to his body. *Oh, yes! Bring on the morphine drip, before my brain explodes.* The light pulsated between the shadows. *Yes, give me more.* The throbbing eased. As the pain diminished, he grew frightened. He felt himself settling into sleep and fought it. Did sleep and darkness and the lack of pain mean death? He forced himself to focus on the light, to remain aware of it, however weak and imprecise its glow.

He felt someone fumbling with his clothes. *Oh, geez, they're cutting the suede jacket! It's a Ralph Lauren tailored-cut that fits me like a glove. Why do you have to cut it? Can't you just slip it off, arm by arm? You can move me that much without hurting anything. Please! Just ease it off. Don't tear anything. Keep the seam ripper away. Keep the jacket whole. You can see how classy a Ralph Lauren is. Don't damage it at all, if you can help it. Oh, you're not listening! There it goes. Ripped to shreds!* Even as he pleaded, he sensed the irony. It was survival he should be pleading for, not fashion. But he'd paid a bundle for that jacket at City Creek and knew he couldn't afford anything like it for at least a year, or until the styles changed. His slacks were the same, smartly belted, perfect length. *Remove them with care.* The white shirt was okay to destroy. He had a million white shirts at home, and this one probably had blood on it. Let it go.

These first hands were quick and businesslike, utilitarian. Not until later, when he was finally away from the commotion and clatter of the emergency room and in the ICU, did he feel a gentle, caressing hand and know it was his mother. He could hear her sob and feel her press her cheek to his, and an apologetic shame gnawed at his heart. He had been such a disappointment to this good woman who loved him. After his mission she had wanted nothing more than for him to find a nice girl and settle down. "Please, Sam," she had begged as the months went by, "you'll never be happy until there is meaning and purpose in your life, until you have more than yourself to live for. Your toys won't give you that. Your fancy car and phone, where you text and tweet and twaddle but never have a decent conversation—that's not the answer. The Church teaches . . ."

"Oh, Ma," he would respond, "I won't settle for one girl until I've seen 'em all. Can't you understand?"

"Don't nag," his father would say at this point. "He's a playboy and always will be. We got him to serve a mission, hoping it would help him grow up. But he's old enough now to figure out his own life and what he wants. I've never been able to talk to the kid. He's all flash and foolishness. I'm tired of goading him."

"I want him to be happy," his mother would reply, as mothers always do. Sam could hear her now, tenderly cajoling his father not to give up on pushing him toward character and accomplishment. "He completed an honorable mission. There's something to build on."

His father would have none of it. "The world is a shallow place," he said, "and it's time we conceded that Sam's become a victim of it. The mission suited him. It was an adventure, after all, but he's dropped out of BYU twice now and spent his tuition savings on a sports car. He'd just as soon cruise the singles' wards as pause any place where he could serve and do some good. He's a pretty boy and as shallow as a puddle. All he wants to do is play. I'm disgusted. I've got no faith in him anymore."

The words had hurt but not enough to make a difference. His mother's tears had more effect. Because of her, he'd secretly promised himself many times that he'd change, that this callowness was just a phase he was going through. But after the rigorous structure of his mission, wasn't he entitled to some breathing room? It wouldn't last. He'd find his place and settle sometime soon. In the meantime, life had continued to dance around him, as balmy as a summer day. The crossroads never came.

"He's such a beautiful boy," his mother was fond of saying.

"Yeah," returned his father, "too slick and handsome for his own good, if you ask me. He could charm the feathers off a duck, but how long can he glide through life with no purpose? All style and no substance? Why can't he be like Davy? I tell you, Dot, the kid is missing something I always hoped he'd have, the ability to see the big picture, to know there's more to this world than having a good time."

"He's still young," said his mother, "only twenty-five."

"He's self-absorbed," answered his father ruefully. "At twenty-five, he should know better."

These words were fresh, although not said in the present circumstances. Here in the ICU the voices were subdued, mere whispers in Sam's consciousness. His mother held his hand and sobbed, and he felt his father's strong presence somewhere in the room. Lying there, with tubes draining and pumping and connecting him to life, he heard his parents' opinions and disappointments rattling about in his brain, but there was nothing he could do to change things now. His mother's weeping left him feeling loved, and his father, gruff as he sometimes was, bent over him, took his other hand, and refused to let it go. Maybe his father didn't hate him so much after all—or was he still saying "I told you so" under his breath?

The word *coma* echoed among the shadows of the ICU. Sam heard the term distinctly. *Coma* and *comatose* and *depth unknown*. These whispered phrases seemed to be accompanied by a tangible sadness in the room.

"We understand so little," Sam heard. "We'll do more tests, surgery to ease the swelling on his brain. It could be weeks; it could be tomorrow. We never know what might spark a wake-up and the beginning of recovery."

Weeks? Did he say weeks? Oh, geez, I can't do weeks. Mom's tears, Dad's concern. I can't do weeks. I've got to get out of here!

Sam's thoughts were frantic, but they only bounced around the inside of his skull. He couldn't see, he couldn't talk, he couldn't even blink. Occasionally the shadows settled over him again, taking him away from the light, sucking him down to some dark place that he had to struggle to avoid. *Please, God, give me a lifeline. Give me some way to pull myself back! Let me climb. I'm not ready to fade away.*

Time had no relevance. Was it in a few hours or a few days that his brother, David, came? He must have brought Trish and the kids at least once. He heard their voices, heard Trish crying, and the kids, Gwen and Robbie, squirming uncomfortably in their parents' arms.

David.

He had nothing in common with David. David wasn't like their father. He wasn't gruff or condescending about Sam's alleged "immaturity," but he was no kindred spirit. More than three years older, David had never shared Sam's carefree youth, never charged down Provo Canyon on Bobby Fenster's Harley, never taken a nosedive into the fountain at Maple Creek. He hadn't heard Sting pounding in his ears or run into a mosh pit or crowd-surfed at Saltair. Heck, he'd probably never even kissed a girl before Trish came along. No fun, that boy. Always hitting the books harder than the ball. And what had it gotten him? Sure, Trish was a jewel. David had great kids in Gwen and Robbie. But his career? He was a history nerd, for Pete's sake! A special collections archivist, whatever that was, at BYU. Sam had nothing in common with his brother. But here his brother was, bending over him and bawling like a little kid.

It sent pangs of guilt through Sam. He remembered being a jerk about David's job the last time they'd talked. "It's not as dull as it sounds," David had told him. "In fact, I get to delve into things that other people can only imagine. Photographs, old records, journals. We call 'em primary sources, and they're pure gold in the collections world."

"Good grief, dude!" Sam had sniped.

"You don't get it." David had laughed good-naturedly. "I'm a time detective, and it's fascinating work."

"Time detective, huh? Indiana Jones riding a desk. Sorry, sounds like you're a glorified librarian."

"To you, maybe." David had shrugged. "To me, not so much."

"Give me a break, bro."

Yeah, he had acted like a jerk, but he couldn't help it. His brother had grown old. He wasn't exciting and carefree. Now, in a sterile ICU, Sam could feel David slide a thumb across his cheek, the way he would when Sam was sixteen and hoping for a few bristles to prove his manhood. "Nothing yet, Scamp!" David would chortle, flipping him with a towel on the way out of the bathroom.

Those days were gone. *Nothing yet.* With Trish and the kids behind him, David would pull a chair up to the bed each time they came and coax Sam silently, by the force of love alone, to respond. *Nothing yet,* was all Sam could give.

Once it was allowed, Sam, who came from a prominent family, had no end of visitors. He was usually aware of their words and touch, although he couldn't respond. His mother came every morning and then again with his father in the evening after work. David and his family seldom went more than a day or two without dropping by. An assortment of cousins, friends, and ward members filled the halls on Sundays, and Sam was aware of numerous visits by his bishop as well as several priesthood blessings and consecrations.

Good people prayed for him, sang for him, and sent him get-well messages, which his mother taped behind his bed. Still he slept, wide awake but blind in his own dark, locked-up brain.

He became somewhat aware of a routine, a time frame, which included periods of noise and silence, gentle touch and functional maneuvering. He came to understand when people were attending to his needs or simply visiting him, when they were there out of love, obligation, habit, or just circumstance. It dawned on him that these pent-up hours were like life itself in certain ways—noise and silence, daily existence occasionally interspersed with smiles or tears or simple lessons, but mostly just routine. Nothing ever changed too much, except that folks grew up and grew old, and certainly nothing was changing for him now, locked as he was in his own dark skull. His schedule was fixed. He wasn't going anywhere.

Then one day David came at an unusual time, somewhere out of the routine. Sam had a little trouble understanding the visit within the scheme his brain had learned. David seemed to be alone. Trish and the kids were definitely absent, and Sam couldn't feel his father's hand or hear his mother's weeping, as was the case when they were present. They'd been there earlier. He was sure of it. They'd obviously gone home to rest, to dry their tears, to figure out how to face whatever lay ahead for him, for all of them. It was only Davy now, and that was unusual. He never came alone.

"How are you feeling, Sam?" he said. "Are you hangin' in there? Are you wide awake inside, and we just don't know it?"

Now, that was something. David was the one with the insight. Maybe his advanced education wasn't such a bad thing after all. He was right! Sam was awake inside. *I wish I could tell you, bro.*

"I want to share something with you, Sam," said David, pulling up a chair. "It's something from my work that might excite you, get those nerve ends sparking again. I've been thinking about it for a while now, praying about it, even, and I'd like to try it out."

Come on, Davy, give me a break. I can't tell what it is you even do. Spending your days blowin' dust off old books sounds pretty boring to me. I'm asleep already.

"The doctor says that some kind of constant verbal communication might help pull you out of this, Sam. Well, I can't just talk that long, so I'm going to come and read. I know, I know, you're not a bookish guy. The doc says it doesn't matter. The idea is to have some kind of constant flow of words tickling your brain." He squeezed Sam's shoulder, and Sam could hear a catch in his brother's throat. "We thought about setting up some audio discs in here . . . you know, the scriptures or some novel or something, and we can still do that, but I decided I wanted you to hear my voice, Sammy, and not just on a disc. I want you to know I'm here. I figured maybe with a familiar voice and touch, we'd have a better chance of bringing you back."

Sam couldn't physically respond, but his heart was suddenly full. He'd fight with all he had to keep from being sucked into the darkness. He'd keep his head above water for this guy, his crazy brother. He'd go along with anything. And even his brother's boring work had to be more exciting than lying here with nothingness.

"Contrary to what you think, I *do* get out of the office," David began in a conversational tone, as if Sam were wide awake. "One of my jobs is to search out old family histories and diaries and ask descendants to donate them to BYU. There's some detective work there, running down leads and locations. People don't know what they have in Grandpa's attic."

Okay. When do we get to the good part?

"The real bonus is what you come to know and understand when you read these books. I tell you, Sam, it really expands your world."

I like my world the way it is, thank you. At least, I did before I got jammed up in this cubicle.

"The world isn't only geography," David continued, warming to his subject. "The historian David McCullough suggested once that we shouldn't limit our experiences and relationships to only those who share the mortal stage at the same time we do. Millions of people, many generations, have come and gone before us. There were some great human beings right here in this valley before we came along. They lived pretty challenging and interesting lives. Learning about those lives adds depth to our own."

Geez, here we go with the history lesson again. And that word depth—*it's a sign of the boredom to come.*

"You probably won't like this at first." David chuckled. "I've brought an old, early-twentieth-century journal to read to you. It was written by a fellow named Moroni Chadester. They called him Rone for short, like in Mo-RON-i."

Yeah, yeah, yeah. Tell me all about this guy, Rone, however you say his name. Anything to stay connected . . . just try not to be too dry. Sam wasn't sure about the subject matter, but suddenly he yearned to immerse himself in the sound of his brother's voice, to turn words into images, to melt into the solace of time and space, knowing David held out a lifeline to reality.

"Rone Chadester was forty-eight years old in 1915 when he was writing this journal." David took up the book as he began an unrehearsed introduction. "He lived down in Alpine, in Utah County. He was a merchant and rancher. We just have a record of part of this one year and a little of the next. It's all the family could find. But Rone writes fairly well and gives a poignant account. There's even a murder mystery, which is why I thought it might . . . uh . . . keep you awake."

A little dark humor there, Dave? Keeping me awake? That's okay. A murder mystery? I'll take that over those dusty old ledgers and binders I've seen you rooting through. Give it to me, big brother. I'm seeing colors again, Davy. But not that torch of a Buick, or the Viper, or even my Mustang. This time it's a summer sky. Old Mrs. Crocker, my senior English teacher, would say it was as vivid as polished glass. Foothills, peaks, green pastures. I'm floating, Dave. Don't stop. Please don't stop. Keep reading. I'm hanging on your every word.

Alpine

August 5, 1915—There was a ghastly murder yesterday, the first ever in our village. . . .

Moroni Chadester Journal

Chapter 2

The road where Sam found himself was deeply rutted and layered in dust, but it dropped from the foothills where he stood into a landscape that was made for a painter's brush. He spent his first awkward seconds taking in the beauty of the scene, a lush valley of green pastureland with knots of elm and maple trees and a bank of western hills where the sun could slip away in glory every afternoon. But there was a pall over the land as well, a heavy burden of sorrow or perhaps fear. It was palpable, like fog, except this was a clear day, and only in Sam's mind was the gloom apparent.

Dazed and disoriented, he tried to gauge the valley's width and length and determine where he was. His eyes followed the road as it skirted a pole fence, which looped and twisted over several acres, passing an occasional farmhouse, barn, or stable. Nestled in the north was a cluster of homes and businesses centered by a steepled church, although he saw no highway leading there.

Sam wondered how long he had walked and where he'd come from. The mountains above him in the east and south were oddly familiar. He knew he was in Utah. He could plainly see Timpanogos and the cleft of American Fork Canyon from where he stood. How many times had he and David hiked there with their father? It all seemed distant now in time and place, though the peaks were where they'd always been. "But I don't remember ever being *here*," he told himself, looking down into the green valley once again. He suddenly spotted a figure moving about on the roadside no more than fifty yards away.

"Hello! Hey, there! Hellooo! Can you give me a hand?" A young man was waving his arm, trying to get Sam's attention. He stood next to a vintage roadster, a Saxon, black, with silver trim and high, narrow wheels and running boards. It looked crude to Sam, not sleek or shining the way restored cars usually are, but not especially old or broken either.

"I could use a push, mister," the young man called as Sam approached with some hesitation. The fellow looked somehow odd, the more so as Sam got closer. He wore a billed wool cap and suspenders over a muslin shirt that had no collar. His trousers were thick corduroy knickers gathered at the knees where his long socks were tucked. Sam stared quizzically from the young man to his automobile and back again and realized the fellow was looking in the same puzzled way at him.

"Broken down," asked Sam, "or just outta gas?"

"No, she's got gasoline. I don't know why she quit on me, but I need to push her up to that corner, where she can be more off the road." He motioned toward a grassy patch twenty-five yards away where the fence turned and left a swath of space as it looped around. Leaning forward, he held out his hand to Sam. "John Chadester," he said with a firm grip.

"I'm Sam . . . Sam Carroll, and I'm guessin' this car is one sweet ride!"

Chadester looked at the roadster and then back at Sam as if his words were a little odd. Then he smiled, suddenly understanding and happily taking in the praise. He was sandy haired, square jawed, and wore a dimpled grin. "Yeah, ain't she swell? Got her in Salt Lake last week for four hundred dollars, if you can believe it. My entire savings over two summers. My old man wasn't too happy with me, let me tell ya, but I caught him tinkering around later that first night, checking the engine, fiddling with the lights. I think he likes it more than he's willing to admit. These little buggies are the wave of the future, and everybody knows it. Her top speed'll beat my favorite horse."

"Four hundred? You got to be kidding me."

"Yeah, it was an awful lot to pay, especially if it's gonna keep quittin' on me like this." Chadester shrugged. "Give me a hand, will ya?" He leaned against the square back end of the car, and Sam, still puzzled, joined him. Together they pushed the dead Saxon along the wheel ruts and made good progress toward the grassy swath.

When they straightened up a moment to rest, Sam was still eyeing the classic automobile and its owner with a bewildered curiosity. "I can't believe you got this mint-condition roadster for four hundred dollars. Is it a replica or an original?"

"What do you mean, a replica?" John Chadester bristled. "It's a Saxon. Are you tellin' me I got snookered?"

"No, no, I didn't mean to . . . Heck, even a replica would cost ten times more. No, four hundred dollars is a steal; that's for sure."

John Chadester scowled at Sam again and gave him another once-over. "Who are you, anyhow, and how come you're dressed like that? You come from a circus or something?"

Sam looked down at himself, zippered suede jacket, trim slacks. *What was with this kid? He was the one who looked like he belonged in a vintage sideshow. Knickers? Four hundred dollars for a classic roadster? What kind of joke was he trying to pull?*

"I don't mean to be a heel," said John Chadester, suddenly apologetic. "We had a fellow murdered here last night, and it's put us all on edge when it comes to strangers."

"A murder? Around here?" Sam raised his eyebrows. "Place looks mighty peaceful to me."

"It usually is . . . peaceful, I mean. Nowhere prettier or more peaceful than Alpine, Utah. I guess that's why we're all a little dazed this morning."

Sam suddenly grew weak. His brain began to ache again. His body trembled. Pulsating colors filled his line of vision. The sky above him grew as vivid as blue velvet, but the horizons were dim and ill defined. For a moment he seemed to be floating outside himself, relieved of all pain, and the pleasant sensation made him wonder if he had died and entered paradise. Then he thought he heard David's voice, smooth and even and articulate.

What was he saying? What were the words?

Before Sam could find clarity, the voice changed. It wasn't David but John Chadester speaking with some alarm. "Hey, are you all right, pal?" Chadester was shaking him. "What's happening to you?"

For a few moments, Sam remained in a trance-like state, staring at the winding road and the fence and the green fields, astonishment written on his face. His awareness fluctuated back and forth between two realms of reality. Slowly, he found himself becoming more connected to one, more distant from the other. He swayed a little and then found balance. The rural environment, with its vintage car and country road and mountain peaks, became crystal clear to him again.

"Did you have some kind of seizure?" Chadester offered his hand. "For a minute there, I thought you might keel over."

"No, I'm okay," Sam sputtered. Uneasily, he clutched Chadester's wrist and held on, trying to catch up with reality.

"What happened?"

"I don't know," Sam lied a little. He did know. At least, it was beginning to dawn on him. "What year is this?"

"Why, it's August 1915," laughed Chadester. "What? Have you lost your memory too? I reckon we'll all remember this date here in Alpine. The killing's shocked us pretty good, like I been sayin'."

Sam slipped down to the ground and put his head in his hands. He could feel the breeze in his hair and in the grass where he sat. "It's that old book David's reading to me," he murmured to himself. "My brain's locked in or something."

"What?" said John Chadester.

"Nothing. I skipped breakfast this morning. I just got dizzy there for a minute."

David, you old scoundrel. When you talked about 'getting into history' you really meant it, didn't you?

"Are you having some kind of seizure problem?" Chadester still wasn't convinced his new companion was all right.

"No, I'm fine. I really am." Whatever was happening to him, Sam decided to accept it. He felt better now. He wasn't dead. He had yearned to immerse himself into whatever David read to him; well, now he was doing just that. He would go with it. He would let this experience flow over him, as if it were real, which it indeed seemed to be. Maybe it would make him whole again.

First he needed to get this Chadester guy to stop thinking he had some kind of a problem. He had to take the focus off himself. "You say someone's been murdered? Here?"

"George Sullivan. Just last night." Chadester helped Sam to his feet. "Found him in his barn over across that far pasture. Stabbed, the doctor said. There was lots of blood, but they never found no weapon."

"Someone have a grudge against the guy?" Sam was still trying to regain his equilibrium, but talk of this crime excited him. His brain, his very existence, was clearly connecting to whatever David was reading.

"Not that anybody knows. Everyone liked Sullivan." John Chadester eyed Sam suspiciously again. Then his expression changed, and he added with some shame, "You were acting kind of funny, mister, but it's wrong of me to suspect you just 'cause you're a stranger and have weird clothes. Like I said, everyone is kind of wary, deciding who to trust."

"Let's get back to pushing that car," Sam changed the subject, "before you decide I'm some kind of a wimp."

"I don't know exactly what a wimp is, but I can guess."

Now Sam touched the Saxon with a newfound reverence. The black paint was dull and crudely applied. The frame was heavy. The tires looked like bicycle wheels. Compared to his sleek Mustang, this was a misshapen bucket of bolts that would probably cause John Chadester no end of trouble. And yet, Sam's curiosity and appreciation for cars—all cars—overcame him. By the time they reached the corner and stopped in the swath of grass, he had admired the Saxon from its headlights to its flimsy vented hood. "You say you paid four hundred dollars for this?" he nodded to John as they both straightened up and paused for breath. "Tell your kids and grandkids to keep it running, shine it up, and never let it go. It'll be worth a whole lot more one day."

"Oh, sure." John chuckled. "And I got a lame horse up yonder you can buy for cheap."

The two of them leaned against the side of the Saxon, strong young men sweating over their labor. John took off his cap and wiped his brow with his sleeve. He was sunburned and full of youth. He put his foot on the running board of the car and let his eyes sweep over the two-seat interior. Sam could tell the guy was proud of the car in spite of the trouble and was probably wishing he could show it off.

Sam nodded approvingly. "You've got more car here than you know."

"She's a beauty, all right," said John, who was suddenly squinting toward the curve in the road. "And here comes another beauty."

Riding leisurely toward them on a dappled colt was a young woman in a white shirt that opened at the throat. Her hair, the color of honey, was loosely braided into one long strand that hung down her back. A wide, flat-brimmed straw hat, tied by a ribbon under her chin, had fallen to her shoulder. Though she straddled the horse, she wore a ruffled, cream-colored skirt which dropped pleasingly on either side, obscuring all but her Sunday boots, a shiny pair that suited her.

"Hellooo, Johnny." She waved and approached with warm blue eyes and a shy smile directed more toward the unfamiliar face than the one she knew.

Sam was speechless. She was, without a doubt, the most beautiful creature he had ever seen, and if he'd entertained any doubts about playing along with this fantasy, he forgot them now. *Thank you, Brother Davy!*

John Chadester stepped from behind the car. "Hello, yourself," he said flirtatiously, moving toward the girl and grabbing the horse's bit and bridle as the animal tossed its head. But the girl was curiously eyeing Sam, a handsome stranger in a zippered suede jacket and odd-styled trousers. John quickly turned, recognizing her curious gaze. "This is Laney," he told Sam, "Laney Williams, the prettiest girl in all of Utah County!"

"You've got that right," said Sam, coming out of his stupor and nodding toward the girl, who blushed modestly at the praise. "Name's Sam Carroll."

"Where are you from, Sam Carroll?" Laney Williams was obviously trying not to stare.

"Uh, Salt Lake . . . actually, the Sandy area."

"Sandy? So you're a country boy, like John."

"Well, I . . . I actually spend more time in the city."

"Hey, Laney," John interrupted with a scowl, "should you really be out riding alone when . . . well, you know . . . you-know-what's happened?"

"Oh, I'm all right here on the road." The girl's chin dropped. "It's horrible about Brother Sullivan, though. His poor wife . . ." Laney Williams suddenly noticed the position of the Saxon, sitting sideways in the grass. "Oh, Johnny. Is she stalled again?"

"Yeah, 'fraid so. Sam, here, helped me push 'er this far. I'll have to go get the team to drag 'er any farther."

"I'm on my way home right now. I can send Pa back with the Ford."

"Naw, don't bother him. We can handle this all right." John was sheepish around the girl, Sam noticed, embarrassed about the unreliable Saxon. "Sam, here, seems to know about cars," he told her. "He'll help me get 'er goin'."

"Well, all right, then." Laney Williams shot another smile at Sam before she pulled on the bridle. "Nice to meet you, Mr. Carroll." Sam thought he saw a fleeting backward glance as she turned away, picking up a little speed before disappearing down the road on her pretty pony. Her long braid bounced on her back, and she looked fine in the saddle. Both men watched her go and stood staring in her direction long after the dust had settled and the road had taken her out of sight.

"That your girl?" Sam finally asked, as John moved to gather his coat from the Saxon.

"I love her, if that's what you mean," he said reluctantly. "We grew up together, her and me, and there'll never be another Laney Williams in my life. We been best friends since we were kids, and that's the problem."

"How so?"

"Romancin' her would be a little like kissin' my sister, and we both want to see who else is out there, if you get my drift."

"Yeah, I do. I've always liked keeping my options open."

John shot a glance at Sam but didn't answer. They walked along the road until a fenced pasture rose before them, and then a creek bed fringed by trees appeared.

Sam liked John Chadester. He was a straightforward, honest guy who was willing to take an oddly dressed stranger into his confidence, even with an unknown killer on the loose in little Alpine. Sam took off his jacket, threw it over his shoulder, and walked with his new acquaintance down the road, wondering if this friendly fellow was really only a ghost from the past.

John's home was a two-story farmhouse with three dormered windows and a wide porch. A giant elm tree shaded the yard, and the walkway from the road to the front steps curved around a well-kept flower garden. They circled the porch and entered the house through an attached garage, which John called a carriage house. As Sam looked about, he noticed another car, a torn-up Model T, shoved against the wall. Bridles, halters, and saddle gear claimed most of the space. The automobile seemed to be an afterthought, a neglected hobby of the past. A grizzled old ranch hand was rummaging through some farm equipment stacked in one corner, and John spoke to him before they went inside. "My father home, Billy?"

"No, the bishop and your ma are down at Sullivan's. Least, your ma is. I reckon the bishop is conferrin' with the lawmen. A constable from American Fork came this mornin'. Someone's due from Provo this afternoon." Billy eyed Sam up and down from underneath his crumpled hat. "I don't think they've even moved poor George from the straw where he died. They like to wait for someone official nowadays."

John pushed him forward, and Sam stretched out his hand to the old fellow. "This is a friend of mine, Sam Carroll. Sam, this is my uncle, Billy Jones."

"I ain't yer uncle, ya smart aleck whippersnapper." The old man dubiously shook Sam's hand and then made a feeble effort to return to his rummaging. "Uncle, my eye! I got no use for you!"

"Come on, Billy." John slapped him on the shoulder. "You know you love me."

"Yeah, I love ya, but I ain't yer uncle," conceded the old man with a glint in his eye.

"You love me enough to keep another secret?"

"Oh, hallaluya, what's happened now?"

"The Saxon's stalled on me again. It's down at Knoll's Corner, and I need some help getting her home. Round up the harness and a couple horses for me, will you? And don't say a word to Pa. Once we get her home, I can get her fixed up before he knows she's being stubborn with me again."

"Well, ya better be dang quick about it," groused Billy. "The bishop's gatherin' all the brethren to the church at six o'clock to palaver about the killin'. He don't need no worries over yer rattletrap of a car, I'll tell ya."

But John was already in the house. He led Sam through a warm kitchen marked by a four-legged ice box and a silver-trimmed black wood stove with an oven door and hot plates like Sam had seen in old-time photographs. A cozy parlor was anchored by a piano at one end and a set of varnished stairs at the other. John was heading for the stairs.

Sam stopped him as John took hold of the banister. "That meeting about the murder," Sam said, "I'd like to be there and find out what's going on."

"Oh, sure, we'll be there." John looked his new companion up and down. "But first we got to find you some decent clothes. It's a good thing you're about my size. We don't want folks lookin' sideways at you when they got murder on their minds." With that, John took the stairs two at a time and led Sam to his bedroom, a long rabbit hutch of a space with a slanted ceiling and the dormered window to cast it in daylight. There was another bed and chest of drawers tucked away on the opposite side of the room. "You can use my brother Andy's half of the place," said John. "He's on a mission now."

"You're taking me in?"

"Oh, for a few nights anyway," said John. "That is, if you want to hang around. I mean, you said you were interested in that meeting at the church. And, besides, I've got a feeling you could help me with the car."

Minutes later Sam wore a collarless cotton shirt, wool trousers that buttoned at the fly, and thick suspenders to hold them up.

"I don't know where you found them pants you had," said John, "or that coat you had on, either, but they made you look like you was from somewhere far away from here."

Very far away, Sam thought. He was still uncomfortable in his new surroundings, but he was also curious. Curious about this place and the murder that had everyone on edge. He was curious about amiable John Chadester and his sporty little roadster. And most of all, he was curious about blue-eyed Laney Williams and what she would think of his new clothes.

He sat alone on Andy's bed. After pulling on a pair of boots John had given him, Sam began folding his own things. His smartphone fell from his jacket pocket as he was laying it aside. He looked with wonder at the rectangular screen in his hand. It was completely dark. He tapped the button gently with his fingers. He tried to turn it on. Nothing happened. The phone was as dark and as dead as he had felt not many hours before. *No satellites or cell towers around here. I don't know what you've done to me, Davy boy, but I guess I'm on my own to figure out this world.*

"What's that?" asked John, suddenly coming up behind him. "Some good luck charm from Sandy?"

"No." Sam tossed the smartphone in his hands. "And it would be a little difficult to explain."

"Try me," answered John, curiously taking the dark, dead rectangular object.

"Actually, it's a telephone, and a whole lot more."

"It doesn't look like any telephone I ever saw," said John. "Where's the ear piece and the horn you talk into?" He felt around the edges and his fingers caught the power buttons. "What's it supposed to do?"

"Well, you've got to turn it on and keep it charged, but when you do, the entire world is at your fingertips. It's a device of miracles, this little thing. You can talk to people or get text messages or even pictures, and you can send them too. Why, the next letter you write to Andy, he could have it instantly." Sam snapped his fingers. "Just like that."

"You're joking. There's no way that could happen."

"No, it works. Or it would if we had a way to transmit, kinda like . . . radio waves."

"You mean like a Marconi signal?"

Sam was enjoying this. He felt smug and in charge. There were things he knew that John and his hayseed world could never comprehend. He liked showing off. "Marconi, heck!" He laughed. "This little device is a sort of Urim and Thummim or a Liahona. You can see things in it and get information out of it like you wouldn't believe. It's a library, an atlas, an encyclopedia all rolled into one. It's magic. A real crystal ball."

"So show me. How does it work?"

Sam shrugged, not knowing exactly what to say. He looked at the dark smartphone and slowly felt the wind ease out of his sails. "It won't work here," he finally conceded. "There's no network, no connection."

"I don't understand," said John. "What connection?"

Sam knew there was no way to adequately explain the Internet, the web, the electronic miracle of apps, GPS, texts, and Twitter. *My gosh! How do these people live?* Why had he even bothered to tell John anything about the phone? Just being a smug smart aleck, he supposed. He had always taken pride in the slick, modern, fashionable things he knew about. Only this time his vanity had backfired. The dead phone only made him look foolish.

"I thought you said it was another Liahona," pressed John good-naturedly.

"Yeah, well, even the Liahona needed a connection to something greater than itself, and so does this little gadget. You'll have to take my word on that."

John seemed to note the irritation in Sam's voice and stayed silent for a time. He lent his approval when Sam stood before the room's full-length oval mirror, a slick city kid turned country boy, complete with thick suspenders and a billed wool cap. Sam felt awkward, like he was in costume or in some sort of freak show. The problem with the smartphone had annoyed him. At that moment he wanted to break away from this backwoods never-never land and get back to twenty-first century reality, even if that reality was four white walls and a ceiling light in a Salt Lake City ICU.

John picked up the smartphone again and turned it over. "Where'd you get this thing?" he said. "It just looks like a piece of glass or tin to me."

"Yeah, that's all it is," Sam exhaled, jerking off his cap. "Trust me, John; it's a device of miracles. Your great-grandchildren will all have these things someday and won't be able to live without them."

"Could be," returned John pleasantly. "I can't tell how you know that or where you found this funny piece of glass, and I can't fathom what you claim it will do. But I like one thing you said. The part about it needing to be connected to something greater than itself. Pa says we all need that. We Mormons get it through the priesthood, our families, and the Church because they connect us to the Lord and to each other. We're powered by that lifeline as long as we keep the attachment clear and strong. Otherwise, we end up like your gadget here, I guess—full of potential but useless and empty without the energy that flows behind it."

Sam stared at John Chadester, wondering why, a hundred years later, he'd never thought of faith in quite that way.

Chapter Three

"I TELL YOU, WE GOT a killer on the loose among us! It weren't no stranger come sniffin' around George Sullivan's barn." The sentences were sharp and loud and punctuated by the pounding of a fist on the table.

"Now how do you know that, Jim Peavey? Was ya there?"

"There was nuthin' stole, that's how I know. A stranger would come to see what he could filch. A grudge-holdin' neighbor would come for George."

"Now, Jim," said another man, "grudge or no grudge, do you really think any of Sullivan's neighbors would want him dead?"

This set off a jumble of loud opinions from the men assembled at the church that evening. They sat around a long table in an outdated cultural hall, which boasted a small stage at one end, a warped wooden floor, and no basketball hoops. Sam kept a low profile next to John on the back row and noted with interest the dim gaslights, the wavy, square-paned windows, and the black potbellied wood stove in the corner. There were about thirty men in the room, and they each had a deafening opinion. The cold-blooded murder of one of their own had numbed their sense of order. Their voices were filled with anxiety and rage.

Jim Peavey was just about at blows with the fellow at his left when a tailored, broad-shouldered man appeared, striding to the head of the table. He wore a plain wool coat with a fly-away tie and carried his gray, short-brimmed hat. His presence silenced the room.

"That's my father," whispered John, nudging Sam with his elbow.

Sam was already staring intently at the dominant figure with the trimmed beard and the authoritative stance. This was Moroni Chadester, bishop of Alpine, the man whose handwriting filled the musty pages of the journal David read.

"Brethren, let's invoke the calming spirit of the Lord as we discuss this tragedy," he said, and with that, the venerable leader bowed his head and prayed in solemn tones, acknowledging all the town had lost: the passing of a friend and neighbor, George Sullivan, and the innocence and security of which the village was now bereft. "We defer to thee, our loving Father," said Bishop Chadester, "as we work to bring justice to our murdered brother, mercy to his family, and a return of peace to our community. Wilt thou lead us with a wise and gentle hand in all of these endeavors, for we know our destiny lies with thee."

Three men had accompanied Chadester into the room. John told Sam that one of them was the local doctor, a man named Billingham, who had examined Sullivan. He said the two strangers were most likely a detective from Provo and an officer from American Fork. The three of them stood back as Bishop Chadester took charge and questions began to fly.

"What about the murder weapon?"

"Are we sure it was a knife?"

"Are there any leads?"

One of the most vocal of the group was Mick Sullivan, the victim's brother, whom the men immediately forgave for a lapse of courtesy. "You fellas have been here all day, and poor George is still lying in his own blood in the barn! Why ain't ya found out yet who done this to him? What's takin' so dang long?"

Chadester held his hands out flat to settle the crowd. His words were firm but sympathetic and composed. "We understand your anger, Mick, and your frustration. This is a terrible thing. I've got my own fist clenched tight over it. I can tell you that the body's been removed down to Percy's. It's being taken care of. Maybe you ought to go on home and look after Eleanor and the girls. We'll handle things from here."

"I ain't leavin', Bishop, till I hear what's goin' to be done," cried Sullivan, and several friends pumped him on the back as he slunk down in his chair, still fuming. He was a pink-cheeked heavy man with a flat nose and small watery eyes. Sam wondered if his dead brother had been half as jittery.

"I'm going to let Doctor Billingham talk a little more about it," said Bishop Chadester, "but it appears poor George was stabbed, just like we thought, and more than once, it looks like."

There was a general groan, and Chadester paused to clear his throat. "No weapon has been found, but George's bull knife is missing, the one he carried in a scabbard on his belt, and I'd like to ask you boys to keep an eye out for it in your fields and ditch banks. Could be the killer kept it, but it might have just been thrown away. They got methods of reading a man's fingerprints now, you know. I'll let Detective Miller speak to that. There's no doubt that having the weapon might be helpful in leading us to the killer."

Yeah, and so would DNA and a few blood samples, Sam mused smugly from his seat.

"Nothing was stolen, as far as we could determine," Bishop Chadester continued. "George was in his barn finishing up with the evening milkin' when he was attacked. There appeared to have been some kind of a struggle 'cause the milk pail was overturned and the milk splashed all over. Whoever did this stabbed George a second and third time, like I told you, and Detective Miller here says that shows a fit of passion. Well, we all know how much George was liked and how he had no enemies to speak of, so that leaves us with a puzzle. It isn't natural that a stranger sneaking in to steal would kill a man and then leave empty-handed. And a stranger isn't likely to have such malice for a fellow he didn't know, either."

"Are ya sayin' it's one of us, Bishop?" said an innocent little man with a round, gentle face, whom Sam immediately liked. John said the fellow's name was Lester Hawkins and he'd give the shirt off his back to his worst enemy if he saw a need. Johnny began naming all the men so Sam would know them, and most of them were suddenly in a frenzy. "Is there a killer here?" they all cried out. "Are our families safe?"

"That's what I been sayin' all along," roared Jim Peavey. "It's someone among us."

Mick Sullivan was trembling where he sat. "Maybe someone's got it in for all us Sullivans. Maybe George crossed some fellow in a business deal, and now we all got to pay."

Again Bishop Chadester raised his hands and asked for quiet. "Now, everyone calm down," he said. "We've got to be wise and levelheaded here. The truth is we don't know what happened. Detective Miller's come up from Provo to conduct an investigation. He'll be talking to a lot of you. He'll be going through George's ledgers, things like that, to see if George owed money or made an enemy somewhere. Of course, he'll want to know if any of you saw anything unusual last night, anyone who looked like he didn't belong. In the meantime, the sisters are looking after Eleanor Sullivan and the family. I've asked Jack Harper to post someone from the elders quorum near Sullivan's road for the next couple of nights, and I expect you boys to tend to your own as best you can. This seems to be a solitary crime, and I don't think we have to live in fear, but let's be extra cautious until we know more about what we're dealing with."

Lon Miller and the other officer, a strapping fellow named Crenshaw, stepped forward. "Listen," Miller said, "last month we had a similar incident down in Provo. An old patriarch named Jessie Halstead surprised a thief one night in his barn. Took a ten-inch slash down his left arm trying to stop the fellow from stealing a box of black powder. The scoundrel got away, but old Halstead got a good look at him. He'll testify once we track the fella down. Turns out he was a wanted man named Rawley Swisher who's done this kind of thing before—the petty thievin' part, at least."

"How'd you know that, if he got away?" asked someone in the crowd.

"We know it 'cause he left his fingerprints all over Halstead's anvil, where he set the box of powder he aimed to steal. Swisher's prints were in the records, and that's all you need to make a comparison with what you got. It's like Bishop Chadester said. If we can find the weapon that killed your Mr. Sullivan and get good prints off of it, we'll get our man for sure."

"You think it's this Swisher fella, then?" asked Jim Peavey. "Was it him that killed poor George?"

Detective Miller was a take-charge type, Sam noted, who looked a little condescendingly at the Alpine ranchers because they were so naïve when it came to criminal procedures. He was well built, wore a thick mustache, and took pride in his position of authority. "We always look to recent cases when a crime occurs," he told the brethren. "At this point the deed fits Swisher, who we know used a knife to attack a man at night in his barn, and there's been a rash of thieving going on up and down the county since he's been on the loose—folks missing tools and plunder from their barns or wood sheds. But so far we don't know what Sullivan's killer came to steal. Nothing's missing, except Sullivan's own knife, and even a brute like Rawley Swisher don't usually kill without a reason."

Miller paused and stepped back to retrieve a pile of papers from the table behind him. They were crudely printed pages, each showing a reasonable facsimile of Rawley Swisher, who looked dark, wide-eyed, nearly bald, and in his early thirties. Miller passed the pages among the men and asked if anyone had recently seen Swisher. Sam was thankful that he was a youthful twenty-five and had a full head of curly hair, especially when a couple of the elders claimed they might have seen someone who looked like the man in the picture loitering in town a day or two before the murder.

"You fellows don't know what you saw," cried another man. "You're spooked, that's all. What would this Rawley Swisher be doing all the way up here from Provo? We can't go lookin' cock-eyed at every stranger passing through."

"Well, who else we gonna look at?" spit Mick Sullivan. "A stranger done this. Maybe it *was* this Swisher fella, and maybe he'll do it again!"

"We need the murder weapon," repeated Miller. "Like I said, the knife could give us fingerprints that we can trace to Swisher or anybody else who comes up as a suspect. Keep that in mind. We got modern ways of proving guilt beyond a doubt." Miller faced the crowd with proud authority. "We'll get justice for your neighbor. You can count on that."

The meeting began to break up, although Bishop Chadester spoke individually with several of the men, taking a moment to sit beside them, pat their shoulders, and shake their hands. When he reached Mick, he embraced the victim's brother and, in whispered conversation, spent time calming and comforting him.

Sam watched all of this with one eye on John, wondering why his new friend trusted him, a stranger, in this guarded time. But John Chadester seemed in some ways a younger version of his father, open and accommo-dating to anyone who would push a broken-down Saxon up a road and claim she was a beauty through and through.

As for the others in the room, Sam wanted to snub them all. *What a bunch of losers*, he thought, *walking in here with dung on their boots hoping to catch a killer. They don't have a prayer. Look at that fellow from Provo and the other guy. That's all they have? A few flimsy Wanted posters? No medical examiner, no forensics, no database. This poor George Sullivan doesn't stand a chance at justice.*

Sam found himself distracted. This wasn't his town; these weren't his problems. This wasn't even his century, for heaven's sake! He glanced about the room. It reminded him of an old ward house in southern Utah where his father had taken him once. Things were small and simple and primitive. There was no kitchen here, no backboards or court lines for basketball, no curtain to be pushed aside when the chapel overflowed on Sunday morning.

Heavy wooden doors separated the room from the rest of the building, which would be lit by gas lamp in the winter. There was no flame needed now. It was after eight o'clock and still light outside, but the long summer evening was beginning to send shadows through the windows. The sepia tone they cast put Sam into a contemplative mood. What was he doing here? Why did everything seem so real when he knew it was only a coma-driven dream?

John finally noticed him looking about and slid his own chair back. "Come on, let me show you around." They got up and made their way inconspicuously through a side door, leaving the echoes in the room behind them. "This little church was built clear back in the 1870s, I think," said John. "We've fixed it up over the years, and it's always been the center of things—weddings, funerals, worship services. Everything that's important in Alpine usually happens here. I never thought we'd ever be discussing a murder, though. Pa's got a load on his hands this time."

They made their way outside and around three edges of the old brick church, avoiding the backyard, where there seemed to be a chorus of voices. At the main entry, they passed into a small foyer and through the chapel doors. John looked with interest at the hard wooden benches, the varnished pulpit, the sacrament table carefully adorned with engravings of decorative scoops and curls and large Roman letters, *This Do in Remembrance of Me.*

A small organ stood behind the sacrament table and to the right of the choir seats. "A deacon pumps air into the organ with billows beneath the stand," said John. "'Course you probably do that up in Sandy too." He shrugged. "I spent many a dull hour down there when I was a kid, but at least I was out of sight. I could lean back and sleep if the high council fella got dry."

Sam smiled. Some things never changed.

They moved back into the foyer, and John carefully closed the chapel doors behind them. "I've got something swell to show you," he whispered and took Sam to a small hallway and an unlocked door. Beyond it, a long row of narrow stairs wound to the top of the church. Pinches of daylight seeped from somewhere above, and Sam followed curiously as John moved quietly toward it. They were tall, broad-shouldered boys and were forced to twist sideways as they climbed.

John chuckled happily. "It was easier when I was a kid, but wait till you take a look at what's up here."

When they reached a trapdoor at the top, Sam could see that it was pad-locked, and several cracks in its wood panels let in the light from overhead.

"Is this as far as we go?" he asked, as John rattled the lock.

"Heck no! You think I'd bring you all this way for nothing?" He confidently reached up and traced his fingers along a ledge on the wall. Soon he produced a brass key and held it proudly for Sam to see. "No one else knows about this key except Andy and my pa. He brought us up here once after he was made bishop."

John sprung the lock and returned the key to the ledge. The trapdoor opened with a shudder as he pushed it up. Light floated in from several sides as the pair climbed out onto a wooden floor built directly underneath the steeple of the church. Sam could see that the steeple had been latticed about five feet from the base, allowing the light to stream in and a curious eye to look out across the valley.

"You can see the stars at night," said John, watching him take in the view. "Rainwater slides right off the spiral up above, so it never leaks down here, at least not much."

"That's quite a sight," said Sam. He could see all of Alpine and the rugged benches in the east, which soon ascended to rocky slopes and familiar ridges.

"I used to come up here and look out and get the feeling I was a king, a ruler over everything," mused John. "But when my pa called, it didn't take me long to get back to earth. He didn't like me up here when he wasn't around. He was afraid I'd lose the key or break the lattice or maybe fall and hurt myself. So he had a rule about it—me and Andy could only come if he was with us. He put the key up on that highest ledge and said that when we were tall enough to reach it, he wouldn't worry anymore. We could come up here whenever we wanted then." He paused for a moment, taking in the view. "It's kinda like that with all sorts of things, I've noticed. When I was a boy, my father unlocked every mystery for me. Now that I'm a man, he mostly lets me find my own way, hoping I'll remember where he put the key."

Sam nodded, grasping the implication. After a few more minutes, they climbed down to the stairs again, twisted through the floor hole, and pulled the trapdoor shut. John replaced the padlock.

"Alpine has a real mystery now," said Sam, watching him. "What do you think? Did this fellow Swisher kill George Sullivan?"

John shook his head. "Poor Rawley Swisher," he murmured with far more sympathy than Sam expected. "He sure shoulda kept that knife in his pocket at Halstead's place. He's probably just a common thief, and now he's gonna get blamed for our murder here and every other crime that Miller wants to pin on him. Wrong place, wrong time is Swisher's problem."

"That might describe me," Sam reminded him. "I'm a stranger here. I'm a little surprised the detectives haven't noticed."

They had reached the bottom of the stairs, and at Sam's words, John turned to face him squarely. "It's my father who keeps anyone from looking in your direction."

"What do you mean? I've never even met your father—not formally, anyway."

"You're with me, and that's enough." John paused and put his arm across Sam's shoulder as they moved back toward the hall. "My pa's a humble man, but he's got more sway in this valley than anyone who ever lived here. Not because he's rich or stubborn or full of himself on Sunday—he's earned the people's trust. They love him. They know his heart." John spoke humbly, without a trace of arrogance. "He's a righteous man, Sam, a good and righteous man, and someday I aim to be just like him." His voice broke then, and he smiled. "That is, if I can survive my callow youth and a few wayward friends I'm partial to." He laughed and gave Sam a playful shove. "In the meantime, don't tell anyone you're from Salt Lake County. My pa's clout only carries so far!"

Sam playfully shoved him back with pleasure and looked appreciatively behind him at the door to the steps, vowing to remember where the key was hidden. It was a boyish secret John had shared but an intimate one as well, as if it was his way of taking Sam into the family. And whether it was a brother's love he needed at the moment or a father's support and protection, he tentatively accepted these new gifts in this ever more–brilliant world of his imagination.

Sam followed John back into the hall, where the men were still conversing. John took a chair, but Sam lingered for a moment near the entryway. Noticing some activity in the yard outside one of the windows, he slipped quietly to the door, leaving the elders to hash out their opinions about the murder.

Earlier, a woman had brought mugs of hot cider to the men assembled at the table, and now he saw its source. On the back porch, where Sam's tour hadn't taken him, two women were hunched over a hand grinder clamped to a large tin bucket. One held the grinder firmly, while the other worked the handle, crushing pared pieces of ripe apple supplied by two teenage girls. The girls cut the apples on a table, dumped the chunks of fruit into the grinder, and picked out the stray seeds. They seemed to enjoy watching the juice gush out of the spout. In a nearby fire pit, the juice boiled in a kettle along with water, sugar, and cinnamon.

"There's some inside who are missin' their coffee," said one of the women to Sam. "But this *is* the church, y' know, so unfermented cider is all they'll get!"

Sam grinned and nodded. He refused the offer of a fresh mug because someone had caught his eye. Carrying a bucket of water from the backyard pump, blonde braid slung over her shoulder and ribbons now discarded, was Laney Williams, young and slim and brown in the last glow of sunset. She was exerting every muscle to haul the pail.

Hurrying to help, Sam caught the girl by surprise, and water splashed on both of them as they each tugged at the handle.

"Oh, I'm sorry," said Laney Williams. "Are you very wet?"

Sam brushed his pant leg without looking at it. His eyes were too busy looking elsewhere. "No, no, I'm fine," he said. "It's you that got the worst of it, I'm afraid."

"Oh, it's nothing. It'll cool me off." She smiled and let him take the bucket as he awkwardly switched the pail to the hand opposite hers. "You're Johnny's friend, from up by Knoll's Corner. Did you get the Saxon home before the bishop saw it stalled?"

"Yeah, we did, with the help of a couple good horses and one old wrangler."

"Your name's Sam, if I remember."

"And yours is Laney. And how could I forget?"

"Actually, it's Elaine." She grinned. "But John's been calling me Laney ever since we were children, and by and by everyone picked it up." They'd reached the table and the apple grinder, and Sam emptied the bucket where he was told.

The women had just begun the cleaning-up stage of their cider-making. The sun had slipped low enough to turn the remaining minutes of the day to twilight. Wet and disheveled in her labors, Laney Williams had to be the prettiest girl Sam had ever seen.

"You go on home, Laney, before it gets too dark," said one of the women, a Sister Treadwell, who seemed to be in charge. "We can finish up here."

"Are you sure?" said Laney. "It's no trouble to stay."

"No, you run along. I don't want you out late with all that's been going on. You got your pony?"

"Yes, ma'am."

"Then you go on now, and thank you for the help. You're an angel when one's needed, I always say."

Laney glanced at Sam, a little reluctant to leave, but turned and started away.

When she was some distance from the others, Sam caught up with her and followed in stride. "She's right, you know. But you shouldn't go home alone. I'll walk with you and see you safely to your door."

"You don't know how far it is or what you've bargained for," said Laney teasingly. "Besides, I have my horse. He's tethered over in those trees." She motioned toward a grove of mountain ash at the far end of the yard.

"Blast the horse," said Sam. "He can't protect you from Sullivan's 'boogey man.'" He fluttered his fingers in her face to enunciate the word and was instantly sorry when she was not amused.

"You really shouldn't make light of the tragedy," she scolded softly. "Our town has never known such fear and grief, and of course, his family—"

"You're right. I'm sorry. I can be a jerk sometimes."

"A jerk? That's an odd expression. Is that something they say these days in Sandy?"

Sam smiled to himself. "Yeah, they do say that these days in Sandy. And worse, being a jerk is every bit as bad as it sounds."

"Well, I'll forgive you then, if you're willing to recognize your faults and change them." The twinkle in her eye stole his heart.

"Seriously," he pressed, "you shouldn't be out after dark alone, even on a horse. However far it is, the miles will pass too soon with you for company."

Laney looked up at him and paused, her face alight. "They say nice things these days in Sandy too."

It took every ounce of his reserve to keep from putting his arm across her shoulder as they walked. *Now, where did I come up with that line? 'The miles will pass too soon . . .' That's not me. I'm the fly-by-night guy from twenty-first century Utah, not some kind of wimpy romantic. It's David and that book of his. He's playing with my mind.*

When they reached the pony munching contentedly in the thick grass, Laney said its name was Blossom and took a moment to let it nuzzle her hand with its soft nose. She made no effort to mount but merely coaxed the horse to the street with a few tugs on the bridle. "Come on, Blossom. Come on, boy," she said, and the horse followed obediently, nodding its head to the rhythm of its gait. With Sam at her side and the horse behind them, the clip-clop of the pony's hooves filled any silences that came about.

"It's not really very far," she said, "just down this way and to the right, against the hill at the end of the lane. We'll be able to see our lights soon enough."

Sam soon forgot about David and his book, caught up in circumstances and feelings he couldn't explain. Night had fallen. The dome of heaven was star-studded before they reached the turn. The mountain peaks above them were lines and shadows in the darkness. Sam was full of some strange ecstasy over the poetry of it all. Never had he experienced such perfection in a moment. He remained silent for a while, reluctant to break the spell. Eventually curiosity got the best of him. "John says you want to see the world someday, perhaps get away from here." He wondered if she'd ever even been to Salt Lake City.

"I went to the BY Academy last school year," Laney replied. "But I don't suppose Provo is what Johnny means by seeing the world."

"It's a start," said Sam. "Are you going back there in the fall?"

"No," she answered, surprising him. "There are things keeping me at home just now. I don't want to be away."

"Provo's not that far."

"I guess that all depends on what's keeping you at home."

Sam was quiet then, unsure how to respond. As they walked, he found himself studying the shape of her mouth, the angle of her high cheekbones and chin, the casual looseness of her braided hair. She moved gracefully, even though she was obviously tired from hauling water. Her shoulders curved slightly, as if the weariness had settled there. The lane that took them to her yard wound around a knot of aspens, and Sam could hear their leaves whispering in the breeze. He remembered camping with his dad in the high Uintahs and how the trees murmured above the tent at night when everything else was still. His dad had called it the song of heaven, but Sam had never thought much about it. Now he did.

The house was a modest Victorian, a single-level brick home, tall. The roof of the narrow front porch was supported by scalloped posts, and the varnished door boasted an oval window of frosted glass. Sam saw all of this because someone was on the front steps with a lantern.

As they approached, the man walked out to meet them. He was a slight, middle-aged man, whose hair was already turning silver. His shoulders were bent, and his square-jawed features were etched and creased in all the likely places, but in the lantern light, his gray eyes twinkled with goodwill.

"Laney?" he said. "We were watching for you."

Laney kissed his cheek and then turned back to Sam as the man lifted the lantern for a better view. "Papa, this is Mr. Carroll, a friend of John's. He was kind enough to walk me home."

"Thank you, Mr. Carroll." Her father graciously thrust his arm forward. "I'm Kenneth Williams. Everyone calls me Kit."

"Sam . . . Sam Carroll, sir."

They shook hands, and Kit Williams looked again at Laney. "I'll take care of Blossom. You go on in. Joey's waiting up." With that, Laney's father spoke gently to the pony, grabbed hold of its bit, and led the horse toward the barn.

Sam turned to leave. "I'd better be getting back," he said softly to Laney. "John will wonder where I've gone."

"Just a minute; there's someone I want you to meet."

Expecting to see Laney's mother as they entered the house, Sam wasn't surprised when a bell-shaped, gentle-looking woman greeted them with her hands full of the dinner plates she was clearing from the parlor table.

"Oh, my goodness, Laney, you didn't bring a caller at this time of night!" Her laugh was musical, like Laney's, and her disposition warm and kind. But it was another figure in the room who immediately drew everyone's attention.

"Laney!" A young boy who looked like an oversized elf suddenly scooted across the hardwood floor on a little four-wheeled, iron-plated sled. Sam saw immediately that the child had only short, misshapen feet in place of legs and that his large head connoted some type of mental retardation. But he was curly-headed, wide-eyed, and happy, especially at the sight of his sister. Paddling the rolling contraption with his hands, he was instantly there, reaching up to throw his arms around her as she bent to greet him. He was trembling with joy when she finally let him go.

"Joey," said Laney, directing him to look at Sam, "I want you to meet Mr. Carroll. Mr. Carroll, this is my brother Joey, the terror of our house!"

Before Sam could do more than tip his chin and drop to the boy's level, Joey had thrown his arms around him, embracing him as he had Laney, with squeals of laughter that left Sam astonished at this child and his open heart.

Soon Laney had the boy giggling over a peculiarly carved apple she had brought home from the church. Its stem looked like an unruly cowlick above two puffy eyes, and Joey was delighted.

"He's eight years old," Laney told Sam as the boy nodded proudly. "He'll be baptized soon, although he's already near to perfect!" With this, she held him close again, rubbing her own cheek against his and tousling his sunbeam-colored hair.

"I'm very pleased to meet you, Mr. Williams," was all that Sam could think to say as he shook the boy's hand, but that seemed to be enough. Warm affection flooded from the child in return for every piece of attention he received, and because he could not clearly speak, it came in bursts of laughter and moments of innocence and joy.

"Now I know what's keeping you at home," Sam said to Laney. "He must have been miserable while you were in Provo."

"I was the one who was miserable," she returned, smiling at Joey.

Later, after Sam turned down Sister Williams's offer of a plate of food and Laney lingered long enough on the porch to make him glad he'd come, he said good-bye and started back to the church, wondering if John was looking for him. Meeting Laney's father on the path, he nodded and exchanged pleasantries as Kit Williams paused, still carrying the lantern he had taken to the barn.

"I reckon the bishop had his hands full at the church tonight," the man remarked. "Everyone's in a fever over poor George Sullivan and what happened to him."

"A couple of officers were there," said Sam. "The bishop told what he knew and asked the brethren to support the investigation. They're looking for a guy named Swisher, who attacked a man in his barn last month in Provo. But it's a thin connection." When Williams offered nothing back, Sam added, "You couldn't make it to the meeting?"

"That kind of thing's for younger fellows. I got my own to look out for here." There seemed to be deep sadness in the man's gray eyes, as if he was more aware than most of a small town's vulnerabilities and those that belonged particularly to him.

*　　*　　*

"You never fooled me at all!" teased John when Sam found him waiting outside the darkened church. "The minute I learned about Laney being here, I knew just where you'd gone."

"She's an angel," murmured Sam, still locked under a romantic spell.

"I guess you met Joey."

"Yeah, I met him. Laney loves him, the lucky kid."

"He's dying, you know." John was leaning against the front gate in the shadows. "It could be anytime. He's all screwed up inside with a weak heart and a dozen other problems. It's a miracle he's lasted this long, the way he is."

"I've never been one to pay much attention to kids," admitted Sam. "I've got a niece and nephew I care about, but kids in general kinda cramp my style."

"What do you mean by that?" John was puzzled by the phrase.

Sam shrugged, suddenly ashamed. His own self-centered life was so shallow that he wanted to chew up the word *style* and spit it into the nearest watering trough.

"I like kids," said John, as they moved together toward the wagon. "I hope to have a bunch of 'em someday, and if any of 'em needs a little extra help like Joey Williams does, I hope to heaven its mother is a girl like Laney—although I wouldn't wish that kind of heartache on anyone."

Sam stared at his friend. The warm glow of the evening left him, and all he could remember of it was what Laney had said about what was keeping her at home. It wasn't just *missing* her brother; it was *losing* him.

Geez, Davy, what have you got me into here? I see the colors of this world. I hear the voices. I feel what's going on. It's like I'm really living with these people. What's going on inside my skull, David? Just because I'm blind to my own twenty-first-century existence doesn't mean I want to live in another time. Or do I? Those must be powerful words you're reading, bro. They're messing with my brain. They've got me locked into something I don't quite understand, something I'm not sure I want to be a part of—and yet I'm here and becoming emotionally involved. These people, this place . . . keep reading, Dave. I'm not quite ready to give them up.

The Field Is White

August 7, 1915—Worry pervades the town, as the detectives have not found much. Funeral held today. I attempted to assuage the grief and fear. Soon we must turn our concerns to the harvest, with poor George's fate still unaccounted for.

Moroni Chadester Journal

Chapter Four

"I CAN ALWAYS USE A strapping young man like you if you're willing to put in the time this fall," said Moroni Chadester when John introduced Sam. They were standing in the yard following the morning chores, discussing Sam's situation. "Can you handle a hay rake or a baler? Have you had any experience with machinery?"

A hay rake? A baler? What kind of antique, museum-piece machinery is this man talking about? Give me a set of keys and a high-speed stick shift. That's the machinery I know.

"I'll work hard for you, sir," answered Sam, "for taking me in as you have."

"Sam's got his eye on Laney Williams," put in Johnny with a grin. "He'd kind of like to stick around awhile."

Bishop Chadester nodded approvingly, but he also paused to take Sam's measure. Sam examined him as well. Bishop Chadester was a robust man, dignified in stature but managerial in attitude. Sam noted a gentle protectiveness in the bishop toward one particular member of his flock.

"Be careful with that girl," the bishop said finally. "Be a gentleman. The Williams family has enough to worry over with young Joe. Laney is their life. Make sure you mind your manners."

"Of course," said Sam, a bit resentful that his intentions were being questioned.

That morning in John's bedroom he had tried to open up to his new friend without giving away too much. He wanted these people to know that he was worthy of their friendship, that he was worthy of Laney Williams. He wasn't just some lay-about who'd come to town searching for an easy ride.

"Are you sure someone's not giving up his bed for me?" Sam asked when he woke up in the extra bunk where John had let him sleep.

"Like I told you, that's my brother's bed," said John, pulling on his shirt. "He's on a mission and won't be needing it. You been on a mission, Sam?" he'd asked casually.

"Actually, yes, I have."

"Where'd you go?

"Russia." Sam was truthful without thinking.

"Russia!" John stopped pulling on his boots and looked confused. "We got no mission in Russia. What are you talking about?"

Sam began fumbling. "Uh . . . I was just there for a while. The Church sent a few of us in to check things out, but it wasn't the right time. Someday, though . . . Where's your brother, somewhere foreign?"

"He's in the Southern States Mission, and that's foreign enough for him."

"It's different down there, huh?"

"Let's just say there'll never be a temple in Atlanta, Georgia, if you catch my drift."

Sam smiled softly, aware of things this boy would never know. "You been on a mission, John?" he asked, suddenly proud again of his own expanded horizons.

"Not yet. I'll go after Andy gets home, I guess. Pa needs one of us here to help come haying time."

"But you spent your money on that roadster." Sam was beginning to sound like his father, and he stopped himself. *What am I turning into here? I'm not this kid's counselor.*

"Yeah, that's what Pa keeps hounding me about. He'll grumble clear through breakfast if he's heard the Saxon quit again, and I reckon Billy told him. Let's hope his mind's on other things."

It was obvious that there were other things on the bishop's mind, for he barely mentioned the broken-down Saxon when they gathered at the table for family prayer. "Lessons sometimes have to come through bad experience," he told John shortly. "It's money that appears to be wasted this time. Maybe you'll see your folly, before it's something worse." Bishop Chadester had a hard time getting through the blessing on the food, and everybody noticed it.

"Tomorrow's funeral plans are burdening you down, aren't they, Rone?" said Johnny's mother, Margaret, or Meg, as she told Sam to call her. She was a small, matronly woman with loosely tied auburn hair. She patted her husband's arm and reached to fill his cup. "That Mick Sullivan is no good at eulogizing. It'll all be on your shoulders."

"Mick's a roughhewn sort," John explained to Sam.

His father nodded. "Mick's got a mouth on him, but it's used more for profaning. The preaching will be up to me."

"You can hardly blame Mick for being white-hot angry," put in John, buttering his toast. "George was his brother, after all."

"No, I don't blame him for his anger." The bishop cleared his throat and wearily took up his fork. "But it's sad that George Sullivan has no male family member to speak as he's laid to rest. His brother should have lived his life so as to honor George, but we'll be lucky if he doesn't show up drunk."

"Oh, Rone, surely not," said Meg.

"I think we ought to be more worried about who killed poor Sullivan than who's speaking at his funeral," piped John between bites.

Sam caught a scowl on the bishop's face as he looked over his glasses at his son, but it quickly changed to a patient frown. "Yes, that's keeping me awake at night—and will until the case is solved. Besides justice for George Sullivan, I have the safety of the town to think of. Let's hope Miller and Crenshaw do their job."

"Oh, I don't reckon we're not safe," said John stoutly. "Maybe we need to watch out for the women and kids, but I'm not afraid of this Rawley Swisher or any other lowlife coward comin' after me."

"Sullivan wasn't a woman or a kid," his father reminded them. "Evil struck all of us when it struck him."

John pondered this as he dug his fork into his eggs.

"What about you, Mr. Carroll?" the bishop turned to Sam. "As a newcomer in our town, do you think we country folk are sometimes too complacent, too naïve?"

Sam looked up from his biscuits. Asking his opinion was something Sam's own father had never done. "Well, sir, I'm afraid we have a tendency to trust those closest to us, and sometimes that can lead to trouble."

Chadester nodded, rubbing his neatly trimmed beard.

"Oh, Rone," pleaded John's mother, "you don't really think it's anyone we know."

The bishop stood up slowly and pushed his chair away. "My worry is that Sam here is right, that it *is* someone we know, that it's someone George trusted." He continued gravely. "Perhaps our own town is harboring a monster."

John glanced at his father, sensing his despair. "Naw, I'm thinkin' it was someone from the outside. Maybe not this fellow Swisher, but maybe a tramp looking to steal, and Sullivan caught him in his barn."

"That's my Johnny!" returned his father, slapping John on the shoulder. "Always trying to lighten his pa's burdens . . . except when it comes to automobiles!"

Sam felt some pride in the fact that Bishop Chadester agreed with him—or at least took his opinion seriously. Maybe Sam wasn't so shallow after all. Sister Chadester seemed to like him. She was motherly and solicitous and glad that John had a friend to stay for a while. "He's been so lonesome since Andy left," she said.

John spoke a lot about Andy as he and Sam spent the day on horseback covering the bishop's water master duties. Finding that Sam was actually more of a "city boy," John kept the horses at an easy gait, without a breath of teasing over his friend's obvious inexperience in the saddle. "We got one of Andy's little range buster bridles back in the barn that might be just the thing for you," he said. "Horses seem to like the bit. Remind me, and we'll put it on next time. You sit a horse real nice. You'll make a fine rider with the right equipment."

While his father dealt with Percy, the mortician, and Rudger Estes, who dug the graves and set the headstones at the local cemetery, John competently led Sam along every ditch bank in the valley, turning wheels and raising or lowering head gates as required. He pointed out the pastures and the hayfields that various people owned and the houses where they lived, but he always returned to Andy when he got the chance. "I have to say, I'm a little jealous of my younger brother, going on a mission before me," he admitted. "But I'm stronger and better with the hay than Andy, and Pa said he needed me here, at least while he was bishop and had so many other things to do. I guess that can be a way to serve, hauling hay for your old man, so he can be a better father to the ward."

Sam listened absently. Not especially used to horseback riding, he was saddle sore by noon, and whenever the horses broke into a gallop, he was grateful just to keep from falling off the big roan John had loaned him.

And he couldn't keep his mind off Laney Williams. He noticed her house nestled in its clearing south of one of the fields they passed, and he studied it with the advantage of daylight, hoping to catch a glimpse of her. She was nowhere to be seen, so he imagined her there in the distance, waving to them as they rode by.

He remembered that even when she did appear in this time-warp fantasy of his, it was because of the Chadester journal. Then he put that thought away and refused to consider it any longer. Laney Williams was as real to him as a summer rose with all of its blossom in full fragrance. It hurt him that this beauty might be fleeting, like the flower, meant to flourish only for a season.

Chapter Five

THE NEXT TIME SAM ACTUALLY saw Laney was the following afternoon at George Sullivan's funeral. She joined her mother, her father, who carried the crippled Joey, and three hundred other mourners crowding into the chapel of the little ward house, occupying all of the hard wooden pews and overflowing into the yard.

Mick Sullivan was on the front row, in the shadow of the casket, sulking and trembling in his grief. Sam tried to see if he had shown up drunk as Chadester had predicted, but the man spent the hour sobbing quietly into his coat collar, so it was hard to tell.

"He's got no family," John whispered. "He never married. No woman would ever take him on."

Beside Mick Sullivan on the bench, but with a conspicuous space between them, was the dead man's wife, and on her other side three youngsters—two girls and a boy in his early teens. They seemed to purposely keep their distance from their father's brother, as if he embarrassed them. Sam thought the man looked wretched.

Lester Hawkins and Jim Peavey were there, along with several of the other men Sam recognized from the meeting of the night before, grizzled and provincial men, but wearing the finest clothes they had and showing a deep respect for George Sullivan and the words of Moroni Chadester as he gave the eulogy.

"Brother Sullivan was one of us," John's father intoned. "We will not let his widow or his children be left in need. We will not forget the justice due our friend and neighbor in bringing his foul murderer to answer for this terrible deed, for it was a crime against us all."

Sam's eyes drifted to the two officers, Miller and Crenshaw, who were on the stand and whose legal responsibility it was to fulfill the bishop's promise. They sat stone-faced and unmoved. They weren't from Alpine. This family wasn't theirs. They had no emotional stake in the outcome.

From the corner of his eye, Sam found Laney in the crowd off to his right and watched her as she wept at Chadester's words and held her brother's head against her chest, running her long fingers through his hair. Sam felt his heart expand and ache. Like the two detectives, he was an outsider with no emotional investment here. But Laney Williams was changing that. He was beginning to forget that the real Sam Carroll was locked inside his own skull in a hospital room in Salt Lake City. He was sitting on a hard bench in Alpine, and he could hardly bear Laney's tears.

At the cemetery and the dinner afterward, the townspeople flocked around Eleanor Sullivan and her family. Nor was Brother Mick forgotten in the effort to support the bereaved. Lester Hawkins, Thomas Nielsen, and several of the other men maintained a friendly circle around the man, slapping him on the back and trying to lift his spirits, even joking with him about where he would live now that George was gone. He'd often bunked in the same house as George and Eleanor's family, but that was inappropriate now, and the necessity of getting his own place was maybe a good thing.

"You'll have to find yourself a wife now, Mick," roared Nielsen, "a rich widow who won't care about yer ugly mug."

"Or that bottle you like to tip every now and then," laughed Hawkins.

At first, Sullivan took the ribbing with appreciative good nature, but after awhile he grew sullen and began to push his well-meaning friends away. "I cain't rest till I find George's killer," he declared. "If it's that Swisher fella, I'm gonna find 'im." He departed the funeral dinner early, apparently to nurse his sorrows all alone.

"I've got an extra bunk out in my barn," said Jacob Carney, watching Mick slink away. "He can stay there if he wants to and help with the haying. He's a good worker when he's sober, and I owe as much to George." With that, the men moved through the crowd, still murmuring in hushed tones about the tragedy as they joined the overflow of mourners eating dinner in the churchyard.

Sam found Laney and her family sitting in the grass under a flowing elm. Kit Williams stood to shake his hand, and Johanna Williams asked him to join them on their picnic blanket. He sat cross-legged and played with Joey for a while, teasing the boy with some finger play he'd learned on his mission in St. Petersburg, something the Russian kids had liked.

He made a marble disappear between his fingers and hid it in his palm. Joey giggled just as the kids in the little Russian Primary had done. Laney sat watching them with her knees drawn up under a pretty linen skirt. It was topped by a slim, lace-trimmed tunic and a string of pearls. Her single braid was gone, and her hair was pulled back loosely on her shoulders. It was natural and loose and swayed free. Her eyes seemed an even deeper blue when they were sad. Sam had trouble keeping his mind on Joey and the marble.

"John tells me that Bishop Rone has hired you to help with the haying," said Laney, when Joey had finally tired of the game and cuddled up to her, peering languidly at Sam. "So it seems you'll be around awhile."

"How would you feel about that?" asked Sam carefully, making certain Laney's parents were preoccupied.

"I think it's good news if the bishop's making it worth your hire."

"It's worth anything the bishop pays if it means seeing you from time to time."

"There you go, saying lovely things again."

"It's easy when I'm saying them to you."

Laney smiled, a glowing, dimpled smile that left him speechless for a moment. She was not the brilliant, teasing, modern woman he was used to, flippant and cocksure. But neither was she naïve. She knew the game and played along. There was a sincerity in her flirtation that was genuine and kind. Was she just provincial and old fashioned? He didn't want to know. He didn't want to be reminded that she was just an image in his brain, morphed from the pages of a dusty journal. He sat watching as she busied herself with covering some of the dishes and putting the food away. She must have felt him staring, must have been aware of the fire that had begun to glow between them. But she resisted staring back, and when Sam finally turned away, it was only Joey's eyes he saw. Wide and large and focused mysteriously on him, they seemed to see far more than they understood.

They walked together then, the three of them, leaving the churchyard full of mourners and ambling up Main Street as Sam and Laney had the night before. This time Sam carried Joey on his back. The boy seemed perfectly willing to wrap his arms around Sam's neck, as long as Laney was close by.

"He has a real attachment to you, doesn't he?" said Sam, noticing how Joey always turned his eyes toward his sister.

"And I to him," Laney returned.

They moved past the brick and wooden storefronts on Main Street—an implement business, a blacksmith shop, a grain and seed supplier. On the same block as the church was a small seamstress and millinery shop with women's hats and fashions in the window. An all-purpose store farther on boasted a large sign: *Chadester Mercantile and Dry Goods*. It crossed Sam's mind that this looked like a created pioneer village like the one at Lagoon or This Is the Place, but there was nothing counterfeit about these buildings. They were paint-chipped and dusty, and the tools and barrels and grain sacks that were stacked about their doors were actually for sale. The heat that emerged from the fire at the smithy was real, as was the odor from the stable. Sometimes Sam had to blink when he saw a horse-drawn wagon creaking by or noticed the occasional vintage car crawling along the road on large, spoked tires. He was amazed at how few of those there were.

Only the mountains above the town remained familiar to Sam, the summer-brown foothills laced with green shrubs. The peaks formed the same rocky panorama that would one day look down on a burgeoning population, a million homes and businesses nestled in their clefts and canyons—Timpanogos, Lone Peak, Thanksgiving Point—and a modern freeway, running like a ribbon through it all. When Sam looked at those peaks from this old dirt road in Alpine, they were the same as they'd always been—sentinels of the valley, eternal, unchanged, beautiful.

Joey had fallen asleep on Sam's shoulder, so he felt free to ask, "What happened to the boy? Was he born this way?"

"Yes," Laney nodded. "I'm twenty-one, thirteen years older than Joey. After I was born, Mama and Papa desperately wanted more children, but Mama lost three babies in a row by miscarriage. It was really hard on her, and she and Papa had given up. Mama was in her forties when Joey came along very unexpectedly. From the beginning, of course, we knew he had challenges—deformed legs, some kind of mental disability—but we loved him so. Papa said he would carry Joey on his back forever, if the little boy could just survive." Walking beside them, Laney ran her fingers through Joey's hair as he slept peacefully.

"John told me there might be other problems as well," Sam said carefully.

"He's dying, Sam." Laney's hand flew to her mouth, and her voice broke. She shut her eyes to stop the tears. "His heart is weak and growing weaker. The doctors say there's nothing they can do."

Sam had heard as much from John, but seeing Laney's pain was almost more than he could bear. He wanted to cry out, *Laney, there will come a day when children like Joey can be saved! Why, someday children will be able to get new hearts, new limbs, and even help with mental retardation.* But none of these words would mean anything to Laney now. These people of the past were left to endure things Sam had never feared. He feared them now for Laney's sake, because he was falling in love with her.

Why was that happening? He had prided himself in playing the field before, in never becoming seriously involved with anyone. There were other girls in this faraway land that David's book had locked inside his brain. He had seen and heard them, floating on the sidelines, chatting merrily with Laney and with John. Girls pretty enough to catch his eye. But only Laney remained in focus very long. Perhaps his mother's prayers were being answered through Moroni Chadester's journal. Or perhaps it was Laney herself. She was changing him. She was making him care.

*   *   *

Pictures of Rawley Swisher, the fugitive thief from Provo, began appearing on fence posts and barn doors all over Alpine, and soon children passing on the street would burst into frightened tears at the sight of any stranger who even slightly resembled him.

An innocent tradesman from Lehi removed his hat one day in the blacksmith shop and nearly got skewered by Otis Barkley's little nephew, who came at him with a red hot poker because, the boy said, "he was bald and had bug-eyes like the man on the poster." Farmers stopped milking their cows alone at night, and families kept their youngsters close to home. Everyone wanted to know more about Rawley Swisher and if he'd ever been in Alpine. The worst result of the frenzy was an inordinate amount of sniping between neighbors who claimed to have seen the man and those who called such sightings foolish.

"A guilty fella would never come back here!" cried Heber Golby, and cooler heads agreed.

Mick Sullivan remained a wary man, however, and continued to remind anyone who would listen that he intended to avenge his brother's death "as soon as I get a clue to follow."

Bishop Rone knew he'd seen enough when he was called to the home of two widowed sisters who swore they hadn't slept since the killing and blamed the problem on night visions of Rawley Swisher attacking the patriarch in Provo. "If a good man like that ain't safe," wailed one of the women, "what's to become of the rest of us?"

The good bishop paced the floor. "They're spending too much energy on revenge and fear," Chadester told John, speaking of his entire flock. "I've got to channel that fire toward a better place."

*   *   *

On the following Sunday morning, with George Sullivan's murder still on everyone's mind, Bishop Chadester stood at the pulpit in the little church and faced his congregation. "Our hearts are heavy," he declared, "but as much as our souls cry out for justice, we must turn our strength and labor to where it's needed most. The law will look out for the perpetrator of this crime. Brother Sullivan's widow and her children will be better served if we look out for them. We'll be thick into the harvest in two weeks, and Eleanor'll need her hay cut, same as the rest of us. I'm assigning crews to her place every other day until the mowing's done; then we'll go from there. Your own fields can be worked at a slower pace so we can help a widow and her family."

Everyone agreed, nodding and murmuring assent as one body. Then Chadester cleared his throat and straightened his shoulders. Taking the scriptures in his hand, he read with solemn tones from the Doctrine and Covenants, section 123: "'Therefore it is an imperative duty that we owe, not only to our own wives and children, but to the widows and the fatherless, whose husbands and fathers have been murdered under an iron hand.' We'll live by that principle, Brethren," declared Chadester. "We'll keep our covenants. This is the core of the gospel. This is the message of the Master whom we serve."

Sitting in the pew with John, Sam listened to the lines of Holy Writ and wondered why the scriptures had never sounded quite the way they did that night when Bishop Chadester read them. Was it because he'd never known a widow before or someone who was fatherless? Or someone who'd been "murdered under an iron hand"? Well, now he did. The grief in this town was part of his experience, just as much as if he'd actually lived through it.

He looked across the room at Laney sitting with her family, lovely in her Sunday ribbons. The thought of this girl being anywhere near a brutal murder scene left him weak and dizzy. He cared. He cared desperately.

Then suddenly his reverie was interrupted by the voice of Otis Barkley, the blacksmith, who had risen to his feet in response to the bishop's words. "I've got a hay rake of George's down at the shop," he said. "I'll have it fixed in no time and at no charge to Eleanor."

Thomas Nielson was up on the other side of the room. "My boys and me can work at Sullivan's most every day, Bishop. We dropped acreage this year."

"We can bargain with the baler fellow for split time costs on his machine," suggested Jim Peavey, "and chip in for the price of Sullivan's hay."

Heber Golby and Jack Harper, rising together, volunteered their teams, and Lester Hawkins, his hat in his hands, offered "every waking hour" to the enterprise. "I guess I'd rather be helping Sister Sullivan cut her hay than just about anything else a fellow could think to do."

The willing response to Bishop Chadester's call continued until nearly every able-bodied person in the chapel had made some pledge of assistance. Some of the demonstrated charity, Sam knew, came from the insistence of the occasion and the social pressure of one's neighbors, but much of it came from something else. The warmth of brotherhood and compassion filled the room. It flowed from the pulpit to the pews. Sam felt it in Bishop Chadester's words, in the scriptures he'd read and the principles he'd taught, and he knew the others felt it too. He remembered what John had said about people needing a connection to something greater than themselves. The citizens of Alpine had done that through the priesthood and Bishop Rone. Sam didn't think of them anymore as "chumps" or prairie farmers. He was ashamed he ever had.

* * *

The town's strength and labor was required sooner than anyone expected. That very night dry lightning sparked a brush fire in the draw above Heber Golby's place, and soon the flames were charging down the hill, chewing up everything in their path. They destroyed a length of range fence on the edge of Golby's upper field and left two sheds smoldering before an army of firefighters could be mustered. A team of horses pulling a pumper galloped up the hill from town and went as far as the road would allow before they were stymied by thick underbrush and boulders, still too far away from the flames to do any good. Golby's hay was too green to burn, but the fire skipped south like a glowing wraith, engulfing weeds and sage and prairie grass and quickly threatening the barn, where a dozen milk cows bellowed and kicked, and several horses snorted in blind panic.

Awakened by the commotion, Sam and Johnny pulled on their clothes. They grabbed buckets, pick axes, and shovels as Bishop Chadester roared directions. There was no need for phones or fire alarms. Farmers and ranchers rising early to milk saw the red pall from across the valley, and ten minutes after Sam and the Chadesters reached the Golby yard, thirty men and several women had gathered with lanterns to help. Sam recognized Jim Peavey, Otis Barkley, and even Mick Sullivan, lurching forth red-eyed, as he nearly always did when the townsfolk gathered.

In a long relay of many hands and arms, buckets of water were passed from a coulee in Golby's yard to the smoking barn. The full buckets were heavy, so the women took charge of passing the empties along the returning line. Sam soon caught sight of Laney working hard to shove each bucket awkwardly along.

John and his father joined Golby in rescuing the livestock from the barn. No flames were visible at first, but smoke was billowing as the men led the stomping, whining horses from one end and the frantic cows from the other. Some of the animals, wild with fear, balked at all attempts to save them. When Rone Chadester finally managed to pull a stubborn, bawling cow through the ash and smoke, he came out sputtering and coughing and fighting to breathe. He dropped to his knees and watched the cow go lumbering through Sister Golby's garden, totally ungrateful. The ducks and chickens were just as troublesome, squawking and cackling in the face of every effort to save them from a hen house directly in line of the fire. Fortunately the wind turned in time to leave the roosts untouched.

Suddenly Sam felt Laney at his arm. She was wide-eyed and brilliant in the firelight, and soot from the falling ash had begun to blacken her cheeks. "John's in the barn," she cried. "He went in to save the horses, and I've never seen him come out!"

"His father's over there," Sam motioned, "and Mr. Golby too. John was right behind them."

"I'm telling you, he's still in the barn!"

By this time clouds of smoke were rolling out of the barn door, obscuring everything inside. Horses and goats dashed helter-skelter, animals brayed and bawled, voices on the bucket line shouted for more water. Sam looked about, certain he'd see John in the melee. But John wasn't there.

Laney ran to Bishop Chadester's side and grabbed the arm of his coat with both hands. "Johnny never came out of the barn! We've got to help him!"

Chadester was still on his knees, still wheezing. He was too weak to answer, but he heard Laney's cries, and his face twisted, terror-stricken. He lifted his hands, shrugging his shoulders and trying to get up. His eyes were red and phantom-like as he looked helplessly toward the barn. Seeing that Johnny's father could do nothing, Laney worked herself around him and hurried to the barn herself, her dress shedding ashes and her blonde braid bouncing off her back.

Sam caught her from behind and dragged her away from the door. "I'll go," he cried. "I'll find him."

Laney jerked out of his grip, frantic now, and it took all of Sam's strength to hold her back without hurting her. "Let me go! Let me find him!" She beat on his chest with clenched fists, until his words finally connected. Then she went limp and let him pass, watching in agony as he grabbed a bucket, drenched a towel in water, and slapped it on his face before he disappeared into the smoke.

Orange flames were eating up the back side of the barn by the time Sam stumbled far enough inside to get his bearings. Billows of smoke at the door had smothered him, and only the wet cloth kept his mouth and nostrils clear enough to breathe. Once the smoke funnel was breached, he had barely enough air to search for John and call his name. In a hazy patch, yellow in the glow of the fire, he saw his friend on his knees in the straw, tugging on the halter of a panic-stricken colt.

"Come on, we gotta get outta here!" Sam screamed, gagging on the whirl of smoke that pinched his lungs. "Come on! She's burnin' up!"

John fought him off. "Help me with this pony. Get around on his rump."

Sam moved to the rear of the colt and pushed its hind quarters up and forward with all his strength, while John coaxed and tugged on the other end. The horse whined and snorted and tossed its head. Its large, glassy eye staring back at Sam was a mirror of terror.

A loud crash from above sent cinders raining down on them, and the colt jumped forward with a squeal, still fighting but finally on his feet. John ripped off his shirt and tied it by its sleeves around the pony's eyes. Together he and Sam pulled it toward the door. Men with buckets were throwing water on the smoke, and their voices led the way outside, where the two boys fell gasping to the ground, and the little pony fled in fright to find its mother.

Before Sam could straighten up, a scrum of hands and arms surrounded them.

"You made it, boy!" shouted Heber Golby.

"By Jove, you had us worried!" cried Otis Barkley.

Bishop Chadester was pouring water on John's face and pausing to let him sip it when he could give up sputtering. "I told you to let that pony go," he roared above the cheers, "but you never listen to your old man anymore!" With that, Rone hugged his son, and Sam stood by, proud of what his friend had done, what they both had done together. The red and orange flames crackled in his mind for a long time after that.

So many people were pounding on Sam that he failed at first to realize the exact moment when most of the back-slapping faded away and only Laney was there. "Thank you! Thank you! Thank you!" she cried and buried her head against him. Sam wasn't sure if Laney's appreciation was for John's survival or his own, but he didn't care. All he wanted to do at that moment was hold her in his arms forever and run his sooty fingers through her golden hair.

Heber Golby's barn was a total loss, collapsing in a violent, fiery heap not long after Sam and John escaped. For the remainder of the night the men worked with axes and shovels to dig a fire line and protect Golby's corrals and orchard, and by morning a blackened army of tired neighbors trudged home feeling somewhat victorious. The flames were all contained. Three cows, two horses, and a goat perished in the barn, but most of the livestock were saved.

Golby thanked Rone Chadester with tears and a tapping on his heart. "I'll never be able to repay you, Bishop, nor the good folks of this town. Don't tell me we've got a killer in our midst. It just ain't so."

"You thank the Lord, not me," Chadester told Golby. "He saved your animals tonight, and He saved my son. He used the hands of His servants to do it, but it was all because of Him."

Golby nodded gratefully, and the men and women who remained to help pick up the pieces took Chadester's words to heart, proud that God had called on them in a moment of crisis. Lester Hawkins, Tom Neilsen, and Jim Peavey, their faces smudged with sweat and soot, leaned on their shovels and thought of what they had saved. Even Mick Sullivan stood by, looking satisfied with his part in what had been accounted as God's work.

"I guess I owe you," said Johnny after he and Sam had returned home to wash away the dirt and ashes and go back to bed, tired and sore with the good ache of hard-won physical accomplishment. "I stayed too long, fighting with that colt. You probably saved my life."

"It was Laney." Sam was quick to deflect the praise.

"Laney?"

"She noticed you were still in the barn when no one else did. She knew you hadn't gotten out. She wouldn't stop screaming about it until someone listened."

"Laney did that?"

"She practically pushed me through the burning door, right into all that smoke and rubble. She would have gone to get you herself if I hadn't stopped her."

"You're pullin' my leg. Laney had a worry-fit over me?" John was amazed. He lay back on his pillow with his arms crossed beneath his head and stared at the ceiling in the lamplight. "I'm glad we both made it out, Sam, but I'm also glad I stayed to save that pony. I'm sorry I scared Laney, but I gotta be honest, it gives me goose bumps to think she cared that much. You know what I mean?"

"Yeah, I do."

"Dear Laney," mused John, still in a reverie as he stared at the rafters. "I swear she's the best girl any man could ever have."

"It doesn't sound like you're quite ready to give her up," said Sam carefully. "Are you sure you're still gonna look for something else when a girl like that is right here in your own home town?"

John grew suddenly defensive. "Heck yes, I'm gonna look. Laney and I are friends, not lovers. We figured that out a long time ago. And besides, I've got me a girl down in Pleasant Grove, a real sweetie. As soon as I get the Saxon up and runnin', I'm going down there to take her for a ride."

"Pleasant Grove, huh?"

"That's right. Her name is Alice Cahill, and she's pretty as a peach."

"Well, I'm glad. Because I've fallen hard for Laney Williams, and I wouldn't want to be stepping on your toes."

John sat up and looked at him. His boyish grin turned into a soft smile. "She's got ya, huh?"

"I'm a lost cause, I'll admit it. I've never been so smitten in my life."

"Well, hallaluya!" cried John Chadester, jumping up to pound Sam on the shoulder before he dropped back on his bed again and exhaled pleasantly. His eyes were still red from the smoke, but they seemed to glow at Sam's declaration. "I'll bet you're glad you stopped to help me with my car," he murmured, and it was only later that Sam remembered an almost imperceptible sadness in John's voice when he added, "She always was too good for me, anyhow. I knew she could do better."

Chapter Six

SAM SPENT THE NEXT FEW days working on John's 1914 Saxon. He suspected that either the engine had been flooded or the spark plugs fouled by dirty gasoline. Old Billy Jones peered querulously over his shoulder as he removed the plugs and cleaned the cylinders as best he could. John went into town on Tuesday to buy new plugs at Gordon's Service Station, the only filling stop around. A vertical pump with a glass top let him measure out the gasoline. Turning a handle at the bottom caused the gasoline to rise to a marked level on the glass, and gravity flow would send it through the hose to a car's tank.

"Where'd you learn about automobiles?" asked Billy. "They ain't been around much longer than you have, I reckon."

"Oh, I don't know that much." Sam smiled. "The truth is I've never had to change a spark plug in my life or wait on a flooded engine. Something called 'fuel injection' prevents most of that where I come from. Cleaner gasoline will fix a lot of problems too. But this Saxon has a different breed of engine than I'm used to, and I've got to work with what it gives me."

"'Fuel injection,' huh?" Billy scratched his head. Sam's words made no sense to him, and he finally gave up and went away. "Young whippersnapper," he breathed, and Sam couldn't help sending a grin in the old man's direction.

John returned soon afterwards, running the team at a quick step. The gasoline was sloshing, and four new spark plugs rattled in the wagon bed. John jumped off the seat before the horses even snorted to a stop. "I've got to get this baby flyin'," he cried. "Alice, down in Pleasant Grove, won't wait all summer, and I promised her a ride."

"I've got first dibs," said Sam, "and I want to drive 'er. If I get 'er going for you, that's the deal. I get to drive."

"'Course you do. I want to see if you Salt Lake County fellows know how to shift the gears. But then it's mine. We'll run down to American Fork and see a show, maybe, and check out the sweeties at the emporium there."

"I thought your girl lived in Pleasant Grove," Sam teased. "'Alice in Pleasant Grove.' That's what you said."

"Oh, sure." John's face colored. "Did I say American Fork? Pleasant Grove is what I meant."

Sam pumped him gently with his fist. "You're kind of a playboy, you know. Sometimes you remind me of me!"

John laughed. "A 'playboy,' huh? I don't know exactly what that is, but it sounds like something my father wouldn't put up with very long. So let's get this baby runnin' and enjoy the moment. I want to show you what she can do."

They did get the Saxon up and running. Sam replaced the plugs and flushed the dirty gasoline. He felt good doing it. When the engine turned over and purred, the boys cheered together, waving their arms and hanging on to their hats. The car jerked away with a roar as John threw it into gear. Dust whirled under their wheels. John squeezed the horn, and chickens fluttered frantically in the yard. The Saxon rolled away in a flourish, a fine 1914 roadster, John Chadester's pride, and all Billy Jones could do was watch incredulously from the barn and scratch his head.

"I can crank her up to fifty!" John shouted above the bellow of the engine. "Just watch!" John had removed his cap. His thick brown hair blew back off his forehead to reveal his boyish and sunburned face. He was eager and fearless in the little car. Fifty miles an hour, even on a dirt road, was no great feat for Sam, having clocked one hundred in his Mustang once on I-15. But he flew through the dust and sunlight now, enjoying the sound of John's enthusiastic hoots and squeals. Ordinary things that Sam had long taken for granted thrilled this friend beside him, and Sam found a special pleasure in that fact.

It also humbled him. *I'm a pampered jerk*, he told himself as the Saxon lumbered along at fifty, sounding like a wrecking barge.

They covered every road and cross-point in Alpine, passing fields and farmhouses Sam had never seen. They rumbled over bridges and skirted ditches and climbed toward the brush-lined benches where trails were wide enough to pass. They drove down a bowered country lane, where trees on both sides were as thick and full as an enchanted forest and there was no sky to be seen. Sam vowed to return in a few weeks when those bowers turned to gold. Above them, always, were the mountains, jagged and majestic, eternal symbols of home and of the other world Sam knew, a world he was forgetting.

On one upper road, the two friends traded places, and Sam took the steering wheel for the bumpy ride back to town. They made the switch after they paused to look over the valley, not from some high point, for there were no roads that far up, but from a bench above George Sullivan's spreading alfalfa. The August day was bright and full; the green fields were abundant.

When Sam settled in the driver's seat, he was warm with anticipation. The land spread out before him, beautiful and rich, and his fingers were on the gearshift of "one sweet little car." He jammed the foot pedal hard to the floor, and the Saxon leaped forward like a dart.

"Remember," yelled Johnny, "this is a country road. It's got ruts and bumps and ridges. It's not paved flat like those sissy avenues up there in Salt Lake County." They rumbled along, clouds of dust rolling behind them, and Sam had never felt so free.

"I could get used to this!" he yelled at Johnny as they roared down the hill toward home, and even Sam, in his excitement, failed to realize the deeper meaning of his words. He *was* getting used to this place, this time, this world. His own twenty-first-century life was slowly fading from his mind.

* * *

What Sam had a harder time adjusting to was the sweltering, endless, backbreaking work come haying time. The acres of alfalfa were mowed with a long swath blade behind a team of horses. Gasoline-powered tractors were becoming more common in the East and Midwest, but they had not yet come to Alpine. A driver—Bishop Rone, Billy Jones, or Johnny—would perch on the high seat, directing the horses and controlling the blade as it chewed through the grass. The other men followed on foot with sickles and longer-handled scythes, chopping the foliage the blade had missed.

Sam had never worked like this. They started early while the air was still cool, the sky still white, but by noon the sun flamed like a match, and Sam's skin grew red and raw. He wanted to peel down to his underwear, but seeing his companions always fully clothed, he hesitated and then surrendered to what they considered decency.

Blowing grass snuck beneath his shirt and made him itch. It floated
into his eyes and nostrils. It matted in his hair. Sweat smudged his hat
band and shirt and dripped uncomfortably down his back. Worst of all,
his body ached. His muscles cried at night, tightening in pain. His knees
and shoulders grew sore, the cartilage inflamed. "I'm not in shape for this,"
he told himself. But he was determined to keep up with John no matter
what it cost him. He could not live with these people, or himself, if he
didn't do his part, if he didn't contribute to their needs and to their lives.
Initially, he hated seeing the first glimmer of daylight every morning, for
he knew it meant another spate of hard, back-breaking toil, but not for all
the world would he have whined or refused to pitch in. John's opinion of
him mattered, as did Laney's.

After the first few days, his body began to toughen; his muscles grew
accustomed to what he asked of them, and the work became routine and
even strangely satisfying. He savored the companionship of his fellow
laborers. The rhythm of dawn-to-dusk accomplishment became a part of
him.

The day arrived when a long iron rake with giant teeth replaced the
mowing blade. Now the team and driver covered every field again, raking
the grass into common rows for the baler to digest. This time the men
following the rake made certain every clump, every blade of grass, was
piled in its row. They used hand rakes and spades to gather every stray bit
of foliage the wagon left behind. Barrels of water marked the end of some
of the rows, and at these places the crewmen paused to quench their thirst
and throw water on their faces. Sam found himself constantly looking for
those barrels, parched and sunburned as he was.

At lunchtime the men would find the shade trees nearest to their
work and lie in the grass beneath them. There they would watch leaves
flutter and listen to the branches creak, grateful for any breeze. They ate
sandwiches John's mother had made and sometimes fruit and cake. A
bottle of buttermilk, packed in ice, was usually still cold in the bishop's
rucksack. While Chadester napped for twenty minutes, old Billy and the
boys teased one another about who had worked the hardest. "Ya got to
put more muscle into it," Billy would grouse. "You fellas are too skinny.
Ya can't walk five yards without gasping for breath. The world's gone soft,
I tell ya. Why, back in my day . . ."

Sam smiled, hearing the familiar words, and knowing every generation
felt the same.

The baler was a motorized wheel-lift shared by several ranchers in the valley. Crude by modern standards, it was horse-drawn and required a man at the rear to shovel the scooped hay into a cylinder. There the hay was packed and tied and lifted over the top of an open shaft. Every bale slid downward, one behind the next, until each was shucked off to the ground. Sam took his turn with the pitchfork, dumping mounds of hay into the cylinder, doing his best to keep it full and maintain his balance on the tailgate. The shoveling was hard and he tired quickly, but he was grateful for the chance to ride. He guessed the worst was yet to come. The bales, which now lay neatly, row by row across the acres, would next have to be gathered up, loaded on a wagon, and hauled in to be manually stacked. A wooden derrick, part of every Western landscape, would aid in that part of the business. In the meantime, "bucking bales" became more than just an antique term for a city boy who had grown used to touching screens and pushing buttons for his physical activity. Sam heaved and lugged and lifted until his strength was gone. He used a hook. He used a rope. He used John's willing back and arms to complement his own. Together they loaded more than a hundred bales—filling the horse-drawn wagon, driving home to empty it, and then returning to load it once again.

At the end of a week, Sam wondered if he could survive another sun-drenched day. When dark clouds appeared over the western hills one afternoon, he wearily looked at them and saw a blessing, a brief reprieve from heat and hard labor. Bishop Chadester saw delay too, and with the Sullivan fields to finish, he wanted to wrap up this one. "We'll work all night to beat that storm!" he declared and ordered lanterns hung on the baler and on the wagon Sam and John used to haul the hay. "If the rows get soaked, they'll be impossible to bale. The cut hay will take days before it's dry enough to square and bind."

So they worked by lantern light, and by morning, when the sky turned to pewter and the first drops of rain began to fall, the men were slinging the last of three great canvas tarpaulins over the completed stacks. The bales waiting by the derrick had been covered too, and Bishop Rone took his crew home, full of accomplishment and pride and ready to collapse. "We did it, boys!" he shouted. "By the grace of God, we did it!" For a moment he stood with his arms outstretched, blinking into the raindrops. They splattered his face and beard and then intensified. Soon all of the men were soaked clear through as thunder rolled and lightning flashed. The empty wagon became their only cover until the cloudburst passed.

"Hah!" roared Billy Jones. "We worked the tails off you young bucks, didn't we? Who says us old men ain't worth our weight?"

Lying on his stomach there under the wagon, with rain leaking down on every side and the grass beneath him cold and wet, Sam looked out at the covered bales and the fields behind them, shorn and harvested. His friends and fellow laborers were beside him, lying prone and laughing at the rain. Never in his life, Sam thought, had he ever felt so tired and so satisfied.

"You ever felt so good?" asked John, laughing beside him.

"You mean, you work so hard, it's a pleasure just to stop?"

"Yeah, that's part of it, I guess," John said above the rain. "But mainly I'm talkin' about all those bales of hay we cleared today. Could that little box of yours have done that?"

"No, not that," Sam conceded, and John smiled proudly through the rain.

*   *   *

Sam noticed that the other ranchers also managed to get their hay in before the storm, some by several days. Rone Chadester's place covered more acres than most, causing him to finish last, except for Sullivan's, and just in time. Once they began, the late summer rains were usually frequent, especially near the foothills, with light snow possible higher up.

Even during the push to get their own hay in, the men had devoted two or three days a week to the Sullivan fields, so things looked good there as well. By the time the rains came, most of the mowing had been done, and the grass lay in soggy clumps all across the acreage.

"It'll take a couple of days to dry out," said Chadester. "That is, if we get a spell of sunshine. Let's pray it doesn't rain again so we can get to rakin'."

There was still a pall over everything at Sullivan's. The house, the corrals, the fields, the barn where George Sullivan had been murdered—all were shadowed by the loss. Sullivan's responsibilities hadn't ended with his death. The fields needed to be harvested, the livestock needed to be fed, the house itself, clapboard and wood shingled, seemed to be sinking under a weight of sorrow. The family who lived there was diminished physically and spiritually, and the bishop was anxious to do all he could to help them. He visited with the family nearly every day, and as soon as his own hay was in, he took John and Sam with him. They were subdued and silent as they entered the house, and Sam found himself wishing he were back sweating on the baler. He had seen Sister Sullivan and the children at the funeral, but this time, as the little girls sat huddled around their mother on the parlor sofa, and the teen-aged boy, Tommy, stood by, trying to look broad-shouldered for the bishop, his heart was filled with sharper pity.

Eleanor Sullivan was a capable woman. The family's store of food and basic essentials was adequate for a few weeks. The vegetable garden, the cows and hens, and a butchered calf, would supply their table. John's mother and the other Relief Society sisters would help Eleanor bottle fruit and vegetables and smoke the meat for winter. Some of the hay could be sold, once the need of the family's own animals was determined.

But when Sister Sullivan stood to greet them, Sam noticed something he'd missed before. Eleanor Sullivan was pregnant. Her belly, hidden under a black mourner's smock at the funeral, now protruded clearly. A child was obviously expected in the next few months.

Sam and Johnny listened as the bishop discussed with the resilient widow his plans to help. "As soon as things dry out," he said, "the brethren will rake and bale the hay. I'll help you figure out what to sell and what to keep, so you'll come out all right. The Relief Society will be here during the baling, if that's all right with you. The sisters will prepare lunch and dinner for the men and feed them in shifts so the work can continue straight through. You needn't worry. We'll set tables in the yard, and the sisters can cook in the fire pits out there. It's important to get the hay in before the weather turns."

Sister Sullivan nodded gratefully. She was a raw-boned woman who looked like she'd faced plenty of hard work before. Her brown hair was brushed back and tied, but stray tendrils hung around her cheeks. Her eyes were small and sad but responsive and determined as the bishop spoke.

"I also want to have an auction," he continued. "The ward will put it all together. You needn't worry. We'll see what we can raise to help you."

This brought the first objection from Eleanor Sullivan. "Oh, Bishop, it's too much," she said. "The haying is more than enough. I don't like takin' charity."

"Charity is the pure love of Christ," answered Chadester in his rich and soothing voice. "In this case, it's the love of your neighbors too. You'd hardly want to deny them that, now would you, Eleanor?"

The woman shook her head. Tears sprang into her eyes, and she took the bishop's hand. "Words are not enough to thank you," she said, "and I know wherever George is, he feels the same."

With that, Bishop Chadester motioned for John to join him. They led Sister Sullivan to a kitchen chair and stood on either side as she bowed her head. Sam picked one of the little girls off the sofa and put her on his knee. The other children, drawn by his smile, sat beside him, and he tousled the boy's hair in a friendly way to make him welcome. Together they listened as Rone Chadester used the power of his priesthood to bless Eleanor Sullivan in this terrible time of loss.

"*. . . May the Lord God in all His infinite wisdom and mercy bless you with His peace. May the babe growing within you be strong and healthy and a fine reflection of its father in feature and in deed, that George Sullivan will be remembered through this child and the other precious children who bear his name.*"

Chadester prayed for the health of the family, the success of the harvest, the discernment of Sister Sullivan's friends as they worked to meet her needs. But these were the words Sam most remembered: *May the babe . . . be a fine reflection of its father in feature and in deed.* He took them to heart.

"Don't worry about the auction," Bishop Chadester told Sister Sullivan again as they were leaving. "You know, the ward always throws a party once the hay is in," he reminded her cheerily. "We'll sing and dance and eat and have a grand old time. The auction will just be a part of the general celebration, and everyone will be wantin' to try to outdo his neighbor when the totals all come in. Who can give the most becomes a game, and all for the best of causes." He placed his hand on the woman's sagging shoulder. "Together we'll get you through this, Eleanor." He doffed his hat, and Sister Sullivan smiled weakly and thanked him as he climbed into the wagon with the boys.

"I believe we might even have that auction while we're waitin' for the hay to dry," Chadester said, as they lumbered toward home behind the team. "Let's get the word out and start collectin' donations. No use sitting on our hands while the rake is down."

With the bishop's impetus and authority behind them, ward members immediately organized a party and auction in Sister Sullivan's behalf. Council meetings were dedicated to the purpose, and Karl Savage's barn, nearest the church, became the gathering place for all donations. Tools and books and carefully wrapped quilts soon filled the designated corner.

Someone brought a treadle sewing machine and a wash tub with a hand-driven wringer, both incredibly quaint to Sam but swooned over by the sisters in the ward. Lamps and knickknacks and dishes were in plentiful supply, and Jacob Carney's wife donated a painting that was supposedly worth fifty dollars. "It's Timp in a snow storm," she said, although no one could really tell exactly which mountain peak was featured. Otis Barkley's promise of a set of horseshoes was bound to bring in bidders, and Jim Peavey's donation of a brand new Hammond mantle clock from his Salt Lake cousin drew a great deal of attention. Bishop and Sister Chadester gave a young calf to be auctioned, hoping the highest bidder would turn the animal over to young Tommy Sullivan to raise. Somehow, John told Sam, his father would see that such a thing was done.

Sam watched the pile of donations rise and looked forward to the festivities that would accompany it. He was anxious to see Laney. His days spent in the hay had left no time to visit her or even pass her on the road. When she came one day to bring some garden produce to the auction barn, it had been at least two weeks since he'd seen her. Even in this ordinary circumstance, he couldn't have been happier. She was pulling Joey in the vegetable wagon, which creaked over the uneven wagon tracks behind her, with the boy laughing joyfully at every bump.

"Well, look at you!" she cried upon seeing Sam. "As brawny and brown as a lumberjack. One would think you'd been swinging a pitchfork day and night!"

"Actually, I think I've lost a little weight," said Sam, hurrying to help her unload Joey's wagon and winking at the boy, who was surrounded by squash and cabbages and playing "soldier" with a pair of marching carrots. "I'll be as wiry as Joey here if they work me anymore."

"And still as handsome," remarked Laney with an off-handed smile as she picked through the vegetables. She failed to sense the sudden swelling in Sam's heart. Outwardly he shrugged off the words and lifted Joey from his cart, working off his ecstasy by swinging the boy above his shoulders, listening to him squeal and giggle at the gesture. *I love you, Laney*, he wanted to say. Instead he directed his rapture toward Joey, and the boy was happily dizzy when Sam finally put him down, holding him by his hands as he waddled along the ground and then lifting Joey into his arms once Laney started watching them again. He was glad when the boy leaned calmly against his shoulder, fully accepting his friendship and affection. From Laney he wanted more.

"Does this mean I'll see you at the dance tonight?" he finally asked, gesturing toward the vegetables, the Williamses' contribution to the items in the auction pile.

"I wouldn't miss it." Laney's eyes found his. "For Sister Sullivan's sake, that is."

"Of course," said Sam.

Laney hadn't stopped staring. "For Sister Sullivan's sake and my own," she added. "The boys are always so busy during haying season, the girls get lonesome. It's time to have a little fun." She took Joey from Sam's arms and set him back in the wagon. Pausing to adjust his feet and settle him, she kissed his cheek before smiling back at Sam. "Joey would be my date, if he liked to dance, but since he doesn't, I'll need another partner."

"You can count on me," said Sam, "if Joey doesn't mind."

He winked and watched her pull the wagon down the street as Joey clapped his hands. He'd been asked to post himself at the barn and accept the auction items, or he would have followed her. He would have put his arm through hers and accompanied her home, as he had that first night with Blossom, the pony, trotting faithfully behind. It dawned on him that he had never been alone with Laney, never danced with her, never held her in his arms. He vowed to change those circumstances that very night.

Sam mused restively after Laney left. He found himself pondering the auction items stacked in the barn, secondhand contributions for the most part, surely not enough to help the Sullivans very long. The good people of the ward and the community would pay more than the clocks and pans and lamps were worth, just to sweeten the pot, Sam knew, and maybe that was the whole idea. The blessing would fall on Otis Barkley and Dorsey Phillips and Lester Hawkins, and all the other contributors, as it offered some relief to Eleanor Sullivan, a little relief and a great deal of love from people who had no other way to show it.

Later at home, Sam found John in the bedroom rifling through his closet. "You know, it's getting kinda hard for me to keep coming up with TWO pair of pants every time we go somewhere. Two shirts! Two ties! Two coats! Four socks! Just why did I take you in when you had no clothes?"

"I guess you felt sorry for me."

"Yeah, well, you're lucky Andy left a few duds behind and we're both about your size." John laughed and added with a smirk, "And you're lucky I refuse to be seen with anyone who dresses like a bum. My selfish pride keeps you in tailored goods, my friend, and you remember that."

"Selfish pride, huh?"

"That's all it is. My pa keeps telling me I've got to repent, that selfish pride is my greatest flaw. But then, what would a fella like you do for clothes . . . or a good-lookin' gal? My friends have to have the best, you know, or they can't pal around with me. No, sir! I wouldn't be seen with 'em. It's all selfish pride." John had tossed a pair of pants to Sam and soon followed with a clean white shirt.

"You're a real heel," said Sam with a knowing grin. "I'll need those new suspenders, too, if you're forcing me to look good."

John snapped the suspenders at him, laughing, and slumped to his bed, a meditative expression suddenly covering his face. "You know, Sam, I've been thinking," he finally began. "I don't have much use for that Saxon when it comes down to it. It's always quittin' on me. It burns a lot of gasoline. The tires'll need replacing before I even get 'er broken in."

"What are you talking about?" said Sam, astounded. "I thought you loved that car."

"Naw, she's been trouble since I brought her home. My pa was right. She was a waste of hard-earned money." John sat up and leaned to grab his boot. With a soft cloth from his table, he began to rub a shine. "Naw," he repeated, "that car was never one to keep."

"Can you sell her back?" Sam was still incredulous. He remembered the trip they'd taken on the back roads and how the dust was flying and John was hoping to do fifty. It was a rousing, unforgettable moment.

"Yeah, I probably could sell her back and take a loss," John answered casually, still working on the spit and polish, "but my ma and I were in American Fork today while you were tending the barn. We ran into a couple of fellas my pa does business with, and they seemed really interested in my car. Said they've never seen a Saxon like that. No kidding, they gazed over 'er from stem to stern, and they were pretty wild over how she rode. I let 'em take 'er for a try while Ma was finishing her shoppin'." John laid his boots aside and looked squarely at Sam. "It gave me an idea, those fellas being interested in my car that way."

"What are you thinking? You gonna put it up for sale? You might come out ahead, you know."

"Naw." John shrugged. "I'd never come out ahead, at least not moneywise. Automobiles depreciate as soon as you turn the key. But there's another way to get some good out of it." John hesitated, and suddenly Sam's eyes widened. He knew exactly what his "selfish" friend was going to do.

"I'm giving the Saxon to be auctioned." John grinned. "I told Hanford and Cox, my pa's friends, to be in Alpine tonight if they wanted to make a bid, and they promised to show up! Cox has money, and Hanford probably does too. Heck, them competin' with each other might serve to send the bid sky high and land a bundle for Sister Sullivan. You know, Sam, going over there to the Sullivan place really got to me. What's she gonna do, with a baby comin' and those other little ones to worry over? Heck, she needs what that Saxon'll bring worse than I need what I'll lose. Besides, it's a selfish thing. I want to see the look on that Hanford fella's face when Cox beats his bid. Hanford loved that car!"

John began strutting around the room as if he'd discovered gold. Sam looked at him—a tall, fun-loving kid in his youthful prime, but guileless, and somehow more of a man than Sam could ever hope to be. Sam's eyes grew moist. For a fleeting moment, he was wearing his suede Ralph Lauren jacket, and his red mustang flashed into view, but he felt like a beggar next to this old-fashioned farm kid who would never know what it was to own a smartphone or fly down I-15 on a summer day with Bono blasting in his ears.

*　*　*

The hall at the church was ablaze with lights as people began arriving for the dinner-dance and auction. Eleanor Sullivan and her children were the humble guests of honor, and Bishop Chadester made certain the tone of the festivities was cheerful and uplifting. "We usually wait until the harvest is finished before we have a party," he told the crowd. "But this year we've got a baby on the way. Like its family, the little soul is ours to care for. It's gonna belong to this ward, this community. Since we're gonna love that little boy or girl with all our hearts, we couldn't wait any longer to celebrate its coming. Besides," he added pleasantly, "my hay crew's all tuckered out!"

"Not too tuckered out for dancin'!" shouted Jacob Carney above the laughter.

"Nor spoonin'!" said Jim Peavey, and applause ascended as a four-piece band struck up a bit of country rag-time that made John Chadester tap his foot in rhythm and Sam search anxiously for Laney and the Williams family.

Supper was served on long tables decorated with ribbons and fall flowers—beef stew, fruit salad, hot rolls, and relishes. The Relief Society sisters, headed by their officers and Meg Chadester, had done the cooking and baking early enough to join their families when the eating began. Dutch ovens kept the food warm for latecomers and second helpings.

The auction began as dessert was passed around—ice cream, homemade and hand-cranked, topped with fresh berries. When Sam found Laney, she was helping Joey with another dishful. "Sister Nielsen let him turn the handle on the ice cream freezer," she told Sam, "so he thinks he's entitled to a second helping."

"You've got that right, Joey boy!" Sam tweaked his cheek. The youngster smiled up at him with ice cream on his face and proceeded to offer him a large strawberry, which Sam popped in his mouth with ease. This brought peals of laughter from the little boy, who immediately fished in his ice cream bowl for more fruit.

The bishop's counselor, Jack Harper, was conducting the auction. The tools and lamps and produce went quickly, with Sister Chadester's hand-painted china bringing in fifty dollars after Heber Golby's wife and Doris Harper drove the price up with their good-natured haggling. The Saxon was the centerpiece of the evening, parked outside, but represented by the gold knob from its gear shift, which Harper held up in anticipation when everything else had been sold. Hanford and Cox, the two businessmen from American Fork, appeared in time for the auction, as promised, and they brought along some friends who surrendered to temptation and bid on several items they didn't need. When Harper announced the opening bid on the Saxon, there was a general gasp.

"That's Johnny's car!" said Laney in surprise. She looked questioningly at Sam. "John's not giving up his car?"

Sam nodded. "I think he is."

"But he loves that car!" Laney's eyes were shining with admiration.

"He says it's his selfish pride," joked Sam. "He wants to puff out his chest. He also wants to get all he can out of Hanford and Cox."

"Who?"

"A couple of 'swells' that will bid sky high. Johnny's got their number."

Laney turned her attention to the bidding, which was reaching a fever pitch. Sam spent the time looking at her, so beautiful when her eyes were bright and her face was flushed with excitement. So beautiful anytime, really, but at that moment full of life and full of happiness over Eleanor Sullivan's rising fortunes, Sam could stare unheeded. He could trace the outline of Laney's cheeks, admire the shine of her hair, and watch how her hands moved light and lovely on Joey's shoulder and her mother's wrist. Kit Williams and his wife were absorbed in the bidding, and even Joey sensed that something important was happening near the front of the hall. Only Sam seemed satisfied to let the excitement of the war between Hanford and Cox go on without him. What he cared for most was close by. His own fortune rose with the bidding, for he could sit and dream without distraction and pray the reverie would last.

"Sold to Mr. Hanford of American Fork for $850!" the auctioneer finally declared, and the people clapped and cheered as Eleanor Sullivan stood to personally thank Mr. Hanford and Mr. Cox for pushing up the bid in her behalf. Somewhere in the crowd, Sam knew, was John Benjamin Chadester, former owner of the Saxon, anxious to keep a low profile and perhaps mask his tears.

Amidst the happy commotion, suddenly all eyes turned to a side door near the serving table. Lester Hawkins and Jim Peavey were pushing a reluctant Mick Sullivan into the hall.

"Come on, Mick," someone shouted. "This auction's for you too!"

"You're family, Mick. Come on in and have a plate of food."

Mick looked about uneasily, his hat in his hands. "Bishop Rone invited me," he told someone near him. "It's Eleanor's plunder, that's for sure, but Bishop Rone said I should come and maybe have a bite to eat."

"'Course you should," said Jim Peavey, and soon Sullivan was being thrust forward to many handshakes and congenial punches on the back. "Caught 'im hanging around outside just as the cheering started," added Peavey. "George was his brother. He belongs here too."

Lester Hawkins found a chair for Sullivan. "Here ya go, Mick," he said. "Us single fellas got to take our part of every home-cooked meal we can!" Everyone close by laughed and nodded at Hawkins, a likable little man who understood Mick's plight as a bachelor. Soon Marge Treadwell, the Relief Society president, delivered a bowl of stew and a plate of rolls and fruit salad, and Sullivan's friends sat down to keep him company.

Kit Williams, who had viewed the scene, turned and spoke quietly to Sam. "For some reason that man never measured up to his brother. He must feel some sense of survivor's shame just now. He thinks the town is looking at him and saying, 'It should have been him, not George. Mick was the one we could afford to lose. Why couldn't he have died instead of his brother. George was the Sullivan with class.' That's what he's thinking.

It swells my heart to see the boys being good to him. Let's hope it makes a difference."

Sam looked at Mick Sullivan, immensely enjoying his dinner as he chatted with Hawkins and the others. The ice was broken, and he grew more talkative, even boastful, between bites. "Them out-of-town coppers ain't come up with nothing," he said. "I'm gonna have to track that varmint Swisher down myself if we want any justice for poor George. I could do it, too, if someone gave me a gun and half a chance."

"Sure ya could, Mick," agreed Hawkins, patronizing him. "That's all you'd need is half a chance."

"Finding George's knife would make up for the other half," said Jim Peavey, slapping Sullivan on the back. "That way Swisher wouldn't have a prayer!"

"Hah, you got that right," put in Jacob Carney, standing by. "The fella'd be in trouble then, with ol' Mick here on his trail."

The men were trying to be friendly in their own coarse way. Sullivan ate his dinner and accepted their encouragement. When Eleanor Sullivan approached him with a handful of coins, he struggled to his feet, embarrassed and uncomfortable. "Here, Mick," she reached out. "The folks meant some of this for you."

"Oh no, I couldn't take a thing. That's for the children," said Sullivan, embarrassed. But when she pressed, he finally let her drop the money into his hand, closing his fingers quickly.

She turned without saying another word and moved away with her head high and her chin firmly set. There were no warm feelings between Eleanor Sullivan and her brother-in-law, but the woman's pride made her sensitive to protocol, and she abided by it, Sam decided. George wasn't the only Sullivan with class.

When the tables were cleared away and the music began in earnest, Sam realized that his dreams of holding Laney in his arms wouldn't come true on this dance floor. The two fiddles, one banjo, and the little drum played country swing and hoedown rhythms that were good for reel dancing, toe-tapping, and little else.

"Close coupling is frowned on in a church building," Laney told him pertly when he asked about it. "Surely, it's that way in Salt Lake City too."

"Come to think of it, you're right," said Sam, suddenly grinning. "No one dances together anymore."

"Well, we can dance," said Laney, winking, "but in the proper way, and not too close together."

"Thanks." Sam smiled wryly. "My waltz steps are a little rusty, so I think I'll pass. You go ahead and line up for the reel—or whatever it is they're doing."

Laney did just that. Flashing Sam a smile, she joined the dancers forming a line down the middle of the hall. Soon he was watching her weave in and out along the line to the rhythm of the music, her long, ruffled dress flying, the golden braid bouncing off her back. The girls clapped their hands above their heads, the boys slapped their knees in unison, and the four-piece band kept pace with the quickening energy of the tapping steps. From the corners of the hall, the spectators cheered each new girl who went swinging down the line, and Sam caught sight of Joey Williams stretching his arms as far up as they could reach and squealing each time Laney was the featured dancer. Sam understood the boy's excitement. He was feeling a certain ecstasy himself.

Minutes later when the music changed and some of the older couples took the floor, Laney found Sam on the fringes of the crowd. She reached for his hand, but to his surprise she didn't draw him forward to the floor. "Let's get some air," she whispered, and together they slipped into the hallway and through the nearest outside door. It was a starry night. The late summer breezes were still mellow, the surrounding fields rich with the smell of new-mown hay and prairie blossoms. The rugged outline of the mountains was edged in black against the sky.

"You were the prettiest girl in the reel," said Sam, as they lingered for a moment on the porch. He spoke softly, sincerely, and his heart was pounding. "I felt like I was dreaming as I watched you dance."

"You should have joined the line," said Laney. "It isn't hard to figure out what to do. It would have been fun to meet you when your turn came and know you were there to swing me around."

Sam was sorry he hadn't danced with Laney and envious of those who had. A streak of jealousy cut through him. "What about the other boys, those fellows in the line? Are they blind? Surely every one of them has made a play for you at some time or another."

"Made a play?"

"You know, 'hit on you' or—"

"Hit on me? No one ever hit me in my life!"

"No, I didn't mean that, I mean . . ." Sam was tongue-twisted and flustered, like a school boy searching for his words. He was grateful when Laney suddenly rescued him.

"I think I know what you mean." She smiled. "Though you do talk awfully funny sometimes."

They strolled through the churchyard, letting the lights from the windows furnish the glow to guide them. The lilac bushes along the fence still cast a pleasant odor, and the trees above them murmured as a breeze passed through.

They spied John's Saxon as it sat in all its glory, splendidly deserted on the grass. It had done its part and now waited patiently, its canvas top pulled up, for the highest bidder to drive it away and out of John's life forever. Drawn to the car, Sam and Laney circled it together, contemplating their friend's sacrifice and remembering the times they had roared with him down the country roads that crisscrossed the valley.

Finally, without speaking, Sam opened the Saxon's door for Laney, and she stepped in. She sat down, leaned back against the cushioned seat, and watched him come around to the driver's side. Soon they were both staring through the windshield and imagining the flight of the car through the stars around them. Sam took one hand from the steering wheel to fumble with the floor shift, pretending to jam it into all three gears and take off with a roar. The shift knob was still gone, the auctioneer's tangible symbol of the car, but Sam was only going through the motions anyway and didn't miss it.

What he did miss was the old self-confidence he usually possessed with women, the brash and insolent certainty that he could love and leave any girl he wished, that his relationships were for pleasure only and wonderfully temporary and ephemeral.

"I guess this is the last time we'll sit in this car," murmured Laney, stroking the dashboard. "Come to think of it, it's the *first* time I've sat like this at night in *any* car."

Sam laughed softly. "Not me," he said. "I've been in plenty of cars with plenty of girls . . ." It wasn't coming out right. He had meant to say that none of the girls was as lovely as Laney, but he came off sounding like some kind of Don Juan. Suddenly his past embarrassed him.

"Well, I can understand all the girls," Laney responded merrily, "but so many cars, now that surprises me. Automobiles are still few and far between in Alpine. Of course, like the girls, you probably have more of them in Sandy and Salt Lake."

He looked at her and smiled. She had saved him again from his own stupidity, and he loved her for it. "There are a lot of cars in Sandy and Salt Lake," he admitted, "more than you'll ever know. As for the girls, they must be there too, but there's not one left that I remember." He turned and pressed her close to him and ran his fingers through her hair.

She leaned her forehead against his cheek, closing her eyes. "I love you, Sam," she said. "I love you with all my heart. Those other boys you spoke of are good friends, but my time with Joey has turned me toward serious contemplation when most of them still want to play games. It's not their fault; it's mine. I've grown too old for them."

"Thank God for that," Sam whispered, his heart swelling.

"You seem from a different world," Laney said, suddenly looking at him squarely. "Perhaps you're older too, or at least more experienced. You understand my bond with Joey and why everything else has become secondary to that right now. I'm not sure other people do."

I am from a different world, but I've learned some depth in this one.

Reminded of his ethereal status, Sam wondered if Laney had actually said she loved him or if the words were only wishful thinking on his part. Was he orchestrating her responses? And why had there been so little trouble in this romance? What was the old saying? *The course of true love never did run smooth.* All great love affairs were fraught with challenge and heartache, especially the storybook kind, as this one most certainly was. Yet there had been no problems. Not yet anyway. Perhaps his mother's prayers and David's ancient journal were getting him through his ordeal by giving him a reason to survive. Yet everything seemed so real that he couldn't help but grasp the moment, heart and soul. Laney was so beautiful there, comfortably leaning against his shoulder, her lacy dress pale and pretty against the leather of the seat. Suddenly, Sam wanted to leave the car. He wanted to take Laney by the hand and leave the Saxon far behind. "Let's go," he said, sitting up. "This will always be John's car. We need some place of our own."

But it was more than guilt at stealing John's girl and using his beloved Saxon to do it. Sam remembered how often he had kissed and teased the girls he'd known in the backseat of a car. That was youthful, shallow play, and now he regretted it. He wished he'd saved everything for Laney Williams. Now he desired nothing more than to give all his soul to her, and not in the front seat of a roadster. "Come on," he said, helping her out, "I know a place."

He took her hand, and together they stole back into the foyer of the church, finding the obscure hallway to the wooden stairway door. Leaving the music and voices behind, they found the hidden door and the narrow stairs, feeling their way in the dark. "Just hold on to me," Sam whispered.

She gripped the tail of his coat and murmured a sweet reply. "I will."

"John showed me this place once, in the sunshine," said Sam softly. "Tonight we'll have the moonlight and the stars."

They had reached the locked trapdoor, and already the muted glow of a starlit night was seeping through the cracks of the wood. Sam felt above him for the padlock key and thanked John with all this heart for sharing this particular secret. When he lifted himself up into the space inside the steeple, he could see his surroundings well enough to know that the latticed slits would give them all the light they needed. He turned to help Laney through the door and saw her face in the shadows, eager and full of life.

"This is wonderful!" she cried. "Look, you can see Main Street from here, even in the dark."

"Where there are a few lights on, you can make out things from quite a ways." Sam pointed to a farmhouse in the distance. "See, there's the Golby place. He's left his houselights on. I'll bet the fire looked scary from up here."

"It was scary from down there!" said Laney, remembering.

Sam remembered too. He remembered how Laney had thrown her arms around him when he emerged from the burning barn, grateful to him for saving Johnny. Now they would hold each other again, this time as new lovers, with their world literally and figuratively spread out around them. Standing there beneath the steeple of the church, they faced each other, drawn by nature and emotion, warmed by the spiritual fire of their common faith, their trust in one another, their newly blossoming affection. Sam finally put his arm around her and pressed her to him, thrilled beyond measure as his lips found hers. He had kissed many girls before, scores of them, perhaps. But never had he felt like this.

Laney, too, seemed to tremble with a new awareness. "Oh, Sam," she sighed, "what's happening to us?"

Sam couldn't answer. He couldn't speak. He had melted away and grown frail. His entire perception was changing. He held on to Laney tightly. He kissed her again and again. His very soul was entwined with hers. No other woman existed. He belonged to her, and she to him, heart and spirit. What he felt was more than physical passion. It was the essence of all that mattered in his life.

Davy, what have you gotten me into? I can't hear you anymore, even when I try. I'm losing touch. I can't feel anything but this place . . . the here and now. I'm drifting, drifting completely away, and it's all right. It's wonderful. I don't remember any pain, and I'm completely all right now.

*   *   *

When Sam and Laney left the key on its ledge and climbed down the narrow steeple stairs that night, their world had changed. Before a week had passed, she pledged herself to him. She told Sam that for the first time she was fully committed to a man she loved, a soul mate, an eternal partner. It altered everything, she said. How she viewed the day, the week, the season, how she worked, how she studied, how she prayed. It affected her relationships with friends, with her family, and with Joey, in whom she found even more delight, connected as he was to her good fortune.

"I think he senses in his own mysterious way that I'm happier than I've ever been," she told Sam. "He's immersed himself in that happiness like a child dipping into a pond, not understanding why the water is buoyant but floating just the same."

"What about John?" asked Sam carefully. "Joey doesn't fully understand, but Johnny does."

"Of course he does," said Laney, a bit surprised, "and he couldn't be happier for us."

"You told him?"

Laney nodded. "He was the first to know. We've been friends so long, I felt I owed it to him."

"What did he say?"

"He said he should have known better than to teach a city boy to drive a country road." She looked quizzically at Sam. "I'm not sure what he meant by that, but he was smiling when he said it."

"I think I know," laughed Sam, ever thankful for John's sense of humor.

As for Sam, his heart was constantly on fire. Work became a distraction, but also a gift, for he saw it as a way to earn his life with Laney. Time away from her—to eat, to sleep, to worship, to converse with John and his father, to go about his daily business—became a chore, and he began to realize that his maturity was being tested. Life required balance to allow each piece to flourish.

But as Sam learned these lessons and recognized these changes, there was one vital transformation of which he was not aware; giving his soul to Laney had completely altered another aspect of his consciousness.

"What's this black thing?" he said to John one day as the two of them sat on their beds and Sam casually picked up the smartphone lying in one of his dresser drawers.

"I don't know." John shrugged, immersed in a book. "You said it was a telephone."

Sam gave his friend a puzzled glance and fumbled curiously with the object in his hands. "How could this be a telephone? It's got no dial or ear piece?"

"That's what I said when you first showed it to me."

"Funny. I don't remember anything about it."

John chuckled good-naturedly. "There are a lot of things you don't remember now that you're in love."

John was more prescient than he knew. Sam's double life had ended. Laney's kisses had drawn him over, mind and soul. No threads connecting him to modern life remained. His journey into the pages of Moroni Chadester's 1915 Alpine journal was complete.

Fugitive

September 10, 1915—Oh, dear God! Sullivan's murder solved by a tragic circumstance today. How much blood must flow in our grief-stricken town? How much sorrow must we bear? Our daily peace is shattered by violence once again . . .

Moroni Chadester Journal

Chapter Seven

A SPATE OF SUNNY WEATHER gave the men of Alpine the hoped-for opportunity to finish Eleanor Sullivan's hay. It had been mowed before the auction party and lay waiting to be raked into rows and baled. Bishop Chadester assigned a crew of ten men to handle three available rakes and cover the acreage in time to acquire the mechanical baler before it was scheduled for use outside the valley. Sam and Johnny were pleased to be included in the group. To lighten Sister Sullivan's load, the Relief Society organized shifts of cooks to feed the men at long tables set in the Sullivans' backyard. They used Dutch ovens and fire pits and brought fruit and salads from home. Lunch and dinner proved to be cheery affairs, with plenty of food and respite for the laborers.

Sam looked forward to seeing Laney there, serving the biscuits and chili beans. He took every opportunity he could to touch her hand or surreptitiously wink or squeeze her arm, although he was careful to let her have her space. He loved to watch her as she moved along the table, smiling and speaking to each and every volunteer. "Hello, Brother Pratt. I'm glad to see you're feeling better." Or, "Mamie Stuart, my mother won't rest until she gets your recipe for dumplings. She's never tasted anything so light." The two little Sullivan girls had formed a bond with Laney and often hung about her skirts as she worked. Attentive to their needs, she sometimes let them be the first to taste the stew or sample the lemonade. "Too sour or too sweet?" Laney would ask and wait for one of the girls to pucker up her mouth and the other to giggle as Laney imitated her.

"You help draw the crowd with your kindness," Sam told her when they spent a brief private moment together. "Kindness and good cooking will help any cause."

"They come for Eleanor and the children, Sam, not for the food, but you're a sweetheart to think otherwise."

"True charity only goes so far." He winked.

"It goes farther in this town than in most," said Laney, seriously. "I'm always amazed by how we come together in a crisis. We owe that grit to Bishop Chadester and his leadership, I think. He's a fine man, and John is growing up just like him."

Sam looked around and saw what Laney saw. The men and women at the tables in Eleanor Sullivan's backyard were a band of angels, giving bread and goodwill to their neighbors.

But it was in the fields that the community's concern for George Sullivan's children was most apparent. When John appeared the first morning to work behind Jim Peavey's horse-drawn rake, he had Tommy Sullivan with him. Carefully he tutored the reluctant boy in the art of backing up the team and driver with individual rakes and spades, gathering any grass the iron teeth had missed. When the boy hung back, John put his arm around his shoulder, prodding him with patience and example. But he was no wimp about his teaching. "You see these muscles, Tom?" he bragged once to the kid, flexing his sweaty biceps. "This is where I got 'em. In a hay field just like this. That's what rakes are for. You don't become a man by workin' soft."

"I ain't a man," retorted the boy. "I'm just a kid, near fourteen."

"You're the man in your house now, Tommy," said John soberly. "You got to grow up early for your mother's sake."

Hanging his head, Tommy usually made an effort to follow John's lead, beating at the grass the best he could, but he looked eagerly toward his mother's house and the dinner table on the outside lawn. John would often leave him there when the afternoon sun grew too hot for a boy to bear.

"He'll get better as he goes," John told Sam as they traipsed back to the field alone one day, their rakes on their shoulders. "Childhood's important to a boy," he mused, sounding like his father. "I guess we needn't take it all away from him in one fell swoop." He looked at Sam, wise beyond his years. "You might say, that's what the killer did to this boy and his sisters. He took their childhood away. It won't hurt us to give a little back."

Sam sometimes wondered why Mick Sullivan didn't take more responsibility for his nephew. Mick was there with the other men, appearing every morning with Jacob Carney, rake in hand. He was what the others termed a lazy worker, not lean or young or fit enough to really "thrust in his sickle with his might," but willing to back the others with clean-up duties.

"He probably wouldn't be here if Jacob Carney didn't roust him out of bed," John remarked once, disparagingly. "If he was awake, he'd be somewhere nursing a bottle."

"George Sullivan was his brother," Sam pointed out.

"Like I said, he'd be somewhere nursing a bottle."

"He ought to step in to help the boy."

"Tommy'll be better off without him, sad to say." John dropped the subject and continued to "buddy" with Tommy Sullivan on his own.

For his part, Mick Sullivan was always ready to shrug off his lack of initiative. "I'm burdened down with grief," he told his friends, "torn between doing this work for George and chasin' after Rawley Swisher." His friends—Lester Hawkins, Jim Peavey, and the Pratt boys—didn't believe him, and he knew it, but they patronized him and slapped him on the shoulder as they had always done, accepting him for what he was.

By the end of the week, Eleanor's upper field was fully raked, and the baler had begun to scoop the rows of hay into its bed. The men took turns on the mechanical device, one driving the team, another standing on the tailgate pitching the hay into the cylinder. When the hay was cut and bound, the machine lifted each bale up and over a slide, to be dropped on the ground. There, the strongest boys would stack the bales for pickup by a wagon once the row was finished.

By late afternoon on Saturday, the baling was in full progress. Only one section of the Sullivan property still remained to be raked. It was a pasture near the barn that Lester Hawkins and Billy Jones were finishing. Billy was on the rake, while Hawkins trailed behind with a spade. It was light work, a cleanup job, for the section was small and could have been left as grass.

The other men were three hundred yards off, where a slight rise in the property claimed its position under the lower benches of the mountain. From there, Sam paused, leaning on the tailgate of the baler, eyeing the acreage below. In the distance he could see George Sullivan's house, yard, the barn where he had died, and the fields where he had labored. He contemplated all that George Sullivan had accomplished on his place. Now two figures—plump little Lester Hawkins and Billy Jones, nondescript neighbors with nothing more in life but the ability to work and sweat—were raking the last of his hay. Sam was moved by the scene. The towering mountains behind him looked down eternally on the changing of the seasons, the sowing and reaping, the annual rituals of life. One generation would fade into the next, and year after year after year, the earth would give its fruit, even as each master of the field in his own time was buried beneath it.

While he was musing, Sam saw one of the figures below move suddenly and seem to become agitated. It appeared to be Hawkins who was throwing his arms about, and although Sam could hear no distinct voice from that distance, the man was obviously yelling. The hay rake stopped, and the man driving the team jumped from the seat to join his partner. They stood together and looked intently at the ground and then up to the balers on the rise. After some hesitation and discussion, one of the men—Lester Hawkins, it appeared—began running through the field toward Sam and the others, pausing at times to catch his breath, slowing to a lope when his attempted speed got the best of him.

"Bishop Rone! Bishop Rone!" Sam heard him call when he was still a hundred yards away, and even Jim Peavey, driving the baler, stopped its engine, as every man within earshot was drawn to Hawkins, excitedly stumbling toward them.

Bishop Chadester wasn't immediately available. He had gone to town on other business, leaving his counselor Jack Harper in charge. Hawkins's eyes darted about, anxious to tell his news first to Bishop Rone, the local symbol of authority.

"I found the knife!" Hawkins blurted finally, as he closed in, breathing hard and unable to hold his news back any longer. "I was hand raking behind Billy down there in that last section closest to George's barn, and there it was, there under the grass. The mower had missed 'er, the rake had missed 'er. But I found 'er, lying there in the grass, the knife that killed poor George!"

The men eagerly gathered around Hawkins, anxious to hear all he knew.

"How do you know it's the one?"

"Where is it?"

"Did ya bring it up here?"

Standing there was Mick Sullivan, who hung back a bit until he was encouraged to join the circle.

"Lester, here, says he found the knife," Jacob Carney said, pushing Mick forward, "the knife that killed George."

"You can't be sure," said Sullivan gravely. "How can you be sure?"

"Well, I can't be, yet, I guess." Hawkins was still breathless. "But it was a good-sized blade, long enough, and there may have been blood stains on it."

"How could you tell that, after all this time?" questioned Jim Peavey.

"Yeah," put in Sullivan. "That don't seem likely."

"Maybe not," Hawkins persisted, "but I remembered what Bishop Rone and that detective fella said about fingerprints. They can tell a lot nowadays about who's handled things. That's why neither me or Billy touched the knife once I seen it. That's why I didn't bring it up here with me. I left Billy down there watchin' it, and I come runnin' to tell ya." He turned sympathetically to Mick and added, with some hesitation, "Besides, I thought Mick, here, ought to be the one to identify the knife and present it to the law, him being George's brother."

Mick Sullivan stiffened as all eyes turned to him. "What do you mean, *identify?*" he blurted, suddenly offended. "What do I know about that knife?"

Hawkins quickly grabbed the man's hand. "Oh, no, Mick. That's not what I meant."

John, who had been standing by with Sam, suddenly stepped forward, putting his arm across Sullivan's shoulder as his father would have done. "There was always the possibility that George was killed with his own knife," he said. "Lester here's just saying that if the knife he found belonged to George, you'd know it, Mick. That's all."

"Yeah," added Hawkins. "That's all I'm sayin'. Even if ya don't recognize the knife, the fingerprints will maybe tell us somethin'. They could be Rawley Swisher's for all we know."

"Ya think that's so?" questioned Sullivan. "They can really tell who's touched a knife after this long a time?" His eyes had wandered down the hill, where they could all see the hay rake and the team of horses and Billy occasionally waving and then bending over something in the grass. "You'd think any fingerprints woulda been washed away by now, along with the blood," Sullivan added dubiously.

"It all depends," said John. "I hear they can sometimes tell things. It's good we found the weapon, Mick, if that's what it is. We owe it to George, to Sister Sullivan, to all of you, to get justice for him. Let's you and me and Lester go down there and take a look at that knife. I'll grab a horse from the corral there and go find my pa. Meantime, you and Lester can keep an eye on it until we get back. Lester was right not to move it. The law will see to that. Come on, now. These other fellas can get back to work."

Sam was impressed with John, the way he took command and handled sticky situations, sensitive toward all concerned. He had natural skill for a boy not much more than twenty-two. "Shall I come along?" Sam nudged him as the group began to break up and Sullivan and Hawkins turned down hill.

"Naw, you stick here," John answered. "Truth is this knife Hawkins found might be some old rusty piece of table service that's been lying out in the rain for years. The fella has a tendency to get excited over nothin'. I'm just gonna go down and check it out. I'll be back before you fellas finish this row, most likely." With that, he trotted off, hurrying to join the other two, and Sam was left to watch them go and wonder if the murder weapon had in fact been found.

Sam resumed his duties, bucking bales that slid down the baler's trough, ready to be lifted and stacked in a wagon. He liked the fellows who worked beside him. The bales were heavy enough to require two men to lift them, and Jack Harper, a young husband and father in the ward, became Sam's partner after Johnny had gone. "Feels good to get this done," Harper said in an off-handed way, as they shoved a bale into the wagon bed. He had an easy smile. "Next year my boys'll be big enough to help. It'll be nice to work alongside 'em."

Sam nodded. He respected Harper, as he did most of the men he had worked shoulder-to-shoulder with in Alpine. Almost without knowing it, he had become one of them, both in his labor and his outlook. The place and time he'd come from was as distant now as another world, which it was indeed.

"Hey, look at that," Jack Harper suddenly cried, pointing down toward the barn, where, minutes before, Sam had noticed John riding away on a horse, probably borrowed from Eleanor Sullivan's corral. Now, the two figures left by the rake seemed to be in some sort of argument, pushing and shoving until one dropped over on his back to the ground.

"Hey!" Jack repeated, immediately dropping the bale and leaping over the next to make a run down the hill. Sam followed and, with his longer stride, soon passed Jack, dodging furrows and uneven ridges as he went. Behind him, he could hear several others racing toward the point where the hay rake stood and one man lay struggling in the grass.

It was plump little Lester Hawkins lying there, his round and innocent eyes as confused as a wounded sparrow's. A ten-inch blade with a bone handle protruded from his belly. Blood soaked the grass, and Mick Sullivan was nowhere to be seen.

"He stabbed me," Hawkins groaned. "Mick took the knife and stabbed me. I can't believe it. He stabbed me!"

"Easy, now. Just take it easy." Sam knelt beside him. "Don't try to talk."

But Lester Hawkins couldn't stop. He sputtered out the words in pain and shock. "After John and Billy left, Mick picked up the knife. I said we'd better leave it be, so as not to smudge the fingerprints, and he bellowed out that the knife was his but he wasn't gonna hang for killing George."

Sam took off his shirt and used it to cover the wound around the blade. Hawkins was in agony. His eyes squeezed shut, and tears dripped down his cheeks. His hands felt for the handle of the knife, and Sam took hold of them instead.

"I told Mick it would all work out," Hawkins continued to moan, "that no one would blame him for killing George, even if his prints were on the knife. He tried to run away, and when I held him back, he took that knife and poked me with it good and hard. I hardly knew what happened till I hit the ground."

Hawkins was breathing erratically, and Sam tried to comfort him. "Jack's gone for a doctor, Lester. We'll get you all fixed good as new."

The other men bending near added their voices, and Billy came running up, explaining that he had followed John to the corral to help him find a saddle and had no idea Mick Sullivan couldn't be trusted.

"I think I caught sight of Mick crossing that south field just as we were coming down the hill," said Jim Peavey. "It was someone runnin' pretty good. 'Course I didn't know why he was runnin' at the time."

"I can't believe it," said Jacob Carney. "Mick's been livin' in my spare room for near two months now, a stone's throw of my family. It scares ya to think he was the killer all along."

"We was kind to ol' Mick," said Peavey. "He was a drunk, but weren't we kind to him?"

"He was my friend," murmured Hawkins, bleeding in the grass. "I saw him as my best friend, come to think of it."

With that, the men turned their full attention again to Lester, who was growing pale and listless as the minutes passed. Jim pronounced a priesthood blessing on him. Billy carefully held water to his lips. Josiah Pratt pressed a wet cloth to his forehead, and Sam held his trembling, bloody hands until they both fell limp and still. But there was little any of them could do but provide a bit of comfort. By the time the doctor arrived, Mick's best friend had passed away.

Chapter Eight

"THE BITTERNESS OF IT," SAID Lon Miller, upon hearing what Mick had done, "is that they picked up Rawley Swisher last week in Arizona. He'd been there since before George Sullivan was killed, near as we can tell. We didn't get the word until yesterday. If we'd known, it would have opened us up to other suspects here."

Moroni Chadester was livid. He saw only shoddy police work, and Miller's excuses sickened him. But he said nothing, too shaken by the murder of Lester Hawkins, who had been answering a call of service when he died. "Thank God he wasn't married," he told Sam in passing. Tears filled his eyes as he made plans for yet another funeral in the little Alpine chapel.

But Bishop Rone had something else to worry about as well. Scourged with guilt over Sullivan's escape and the death of Lester Hawkins, Johnny spent the next several days in a deep depression. He tended to his chores and assisted the crew as it completed the baling, but afterwards, while the others gathered to discuss what had happened and plan with the law about how to proceed, John disappeared, seeking refuge from the terrible reality and his own part in it. At night Sam would find him lying in the darkness, staring at the ceiling from his pillow. Often he was silent, but sometimes he would murmur, full of self-reproach and blame. "I shouldn't have left them alone together. Mick Sullivan was a slacker and a drunk. How could I have trusted him? I have the priesthood. Why wasn't I more discerning?"

Hearing this, Sam sat on the bed beside him. "You're not your father, John. Not yet."

John clutched Sam's arm. His eyes were blinking away tears. "If my father had been there instead of me, he would have known better how to handle things. He's a bishop. He has the mantle of the Lord. Lester would be alive if Pa had been there instead of me."

"Maybe. Maybe not. And someday, maybe years from now, you'll be there for someone else," said Sam softly. "You and I, we're just boys, John. We're learning as we go. You handled things the best you could, given what you knew."

Sam was aware that his words were sure to be taken lightly by a young man who needed to hear them from just one source, so he prayed with extra fervor for his friend and was thankful beyond words when he heard the door open a little later. Moroni Chadester had entered the room.

Feigning sleep and providing privacy for the father and his son, Sam heard the bishop whisper, "Don't blame yourself, dear boy. You're an honor to me and to the Lord, in all you do. You couldn't have saved Lester. His blood's not on you. It's on Mick Sullivan." Sam knew that Chadester was encircling John in a paternal embrace. "You did your best here, Johnny," said the bishop, "but even when you fail, I love you. Even your missteps are precious because they are stumbles toward goodness and an ever-virtuous heart."

*　　*　　*

"I worry about John," said Laney, sitting next to Sam at Lester Hawkins's funeral. "He's taken this so hard, as if he's somehow responsible."

"He'll be all right," Sam replied, more solemn than ever. The entire ward was again in shock. Hawkins had no family, but every pew was filled, and people stood in the corners and doorways of the chapel. Eleanor Sullivan and her children were again the center of attention as the savagery of her brother-in-law was now revealed.

"I can't imagine Mick hating his brother enough to kill him," murmured Laney. "It's beyond my comprehension. I love Joey so much I'd *give* my life for him in a heartbeat. There's no way I'd take his . . . *ever*."

"*You* wouldn't, but it's not unheard of, brother killing brother. Cain and Abel, for example."

"Jealousy? Do you think that's why he did it?"

"I don't know," said Sam, "and unless he's caught, I guess we never will."

"Oh surely he'll be caught. I won't be able to sleep until he is. It's bad enough to know he was right here with us and we didn't know what he'd done. Poor Brother Hawkins had to pay for us not knowing."

Sam took her hand, no longer reluctant to show his feelings in public. Along with his great love for this girl, he suddenly felt protective. If she couldn't sleep at night, neither could he. If she were the least bit anxious about daily life, he could only feel the same. "Don't worry, Laney," he whispered, there in the pew with his arm around her shoulders. "Mick Sullivan is as far away from here as he can get, and he's gonna stay away. We know his face. He's on the run from *us*. We have no more to fear." He was pleased when she looked back at him with utter faith and trust. It gave him confidence in himself. He was a man with loved ones to protect.

* * *

"Miller and Crenshaw have met with me," Moroni Chadester announced at the dinner table the night of the Hawkins funeral. "They're mounting a search into the western desert to see if they can pick up Mick's trail. They've invited us to go along if we'd care to join them. I told them we'd definitely 'care to,' so it looks like we'll be deputized in the morning, if you boys have no objections."

"Hallalooya!" shouted John, slamming his fist on the table. "'Course I got no objections!"

"Well, maybe I do!" said his mother.

"Now, Meg . . ." Bishop Chadester tried to calm her.

"And don't you tell me that those officers came to you," continued Sister Chadester. "I'll give this house and the land it's sitting on if you haven't been coaxing them for a place on that posse ever since the notion first came up."

Chadester backed off a bit.

"Oh, Ma, it's just what I need," John pleaded. "I had a part in lettin' this fella get away. I gotta have a part in findin' him."

"You and Sam aren't lawmen," said Sister Chadester, agitated. "You're still just boys."

"They'll always be just boys to you, Meg," said her husband gently. "You're a mother. It won't ever be no other way. But they're both men in stature now, and it's up to me to make 'em men in reality. Don't you worry. They can handle this." He placed his hand over hers. The matter was settled, though the mother took no pleasure in it.

Outside, away from the breakfast table, the bishop spoke to Sam. "I never asked you directly if you wanted to come along. John was quick to jump in, but you have no obligation."

"Yeah, I do," Sam answered, "but I'd come along anyway."

*　　*　　*

They rode out from Lehi the next morning, seven of them, counting Officers Miller and Crenshaw and two other deputies who came with them. Bishop Rone had expected the lawmen to bring a wagon for supplies and in case of injury, but Miller made no apologies. "I plan to move fast and quick," he said. "We won't need no wagon."

The Chadesters brought their own horses and gear, including flashlights. Again Miller considered these unnecessary. "We're not looking for Sullivan in a cave," he joked.

Bishop Rone took all of this in stride, saying nothing directly to Miller and shaking hands amiably with all the officers. The Chadesters supplied Sam with two canteens and a Colt revolver. Oddly, he didn't remember ever using any kind of gun before and handled the weapon with awkwardness.

"Don't you shoot in Sandy?" John teased. "Or are they too civilized?"

"Sandy?" Sam wasn't sure how to respond and instead let the subject drop. He had other things to worry about. He was accustomed to riding horses now, but he still felt like a tenderfoot, and he didn't quite know why. Surely, he'd grown up in a saddle just as John had. Why was he so awkward with so many things that seemed to come naturally to those around him? The wilderness between Cedar Fort and Delta was desolate and foreboding to Sam's inexperienced eye, and he wondered if there wasn't an easier way to track a fugitive. Say, by automobile maybe. Something gnawed at him and told him it should be done from the air, but he never could put his finger on just where that thought had come from or how it could even be done, so he let it go. Whatever method they used, he was excited and anxious to do his part. The other men were friendly enough, and their respect for Moroni Chadester soothed any professional jealousy they might have had regarding him accompanying them.

"A rancher outside of Lehi reported a stolen horse the day after Lester Hawkins died," Miller told them as they stood with their horses preparing to leave. "The horse was saddled and packing a rifle. The fellow left it grazing for five minutes while he checked a line of busted fence. When he come back, the big bay horse was gone. He says it wasn't likely to wander past the grass on its own."

"Too bad about the rifle," remarked Chadester.

"Yeah, but we got some good luck too." Miller reached down and grabbed his own gelding's foreleg, bringing up the underside of the hoof. "Rancher says the shoe on his stolen horse has his mark on it, an X right here at the top. If we can pick up that shoe print, we've got a trail to follow." He dropped the horse's leg and brushed the dirt from his hands. "I don't figure Sullivan would ride a stolen pony into any town where it would be recognized. He's got to be headed out to the desert, where he thinks he won't be found, so that's where we're gonna go, with our eyes wide open for that bay horse and its shoe."

"Did the rancher pick up a trail?"

"Naw, by the time he got back with another horse, he couldn't find anything, but he swears the bay would have come home on its own by now, if someone wasn't riding him."

They left Lehi, reining around automobiles and wagons on the street and soon passing the farms and ranches that edged the town. The mountains on this west side of the valley were less jagged and more distant than the peaks directly above Alpine, and the wilderness in between provided a panorama of sagebrush and juniper as far as the eye could see. Utah Lake shimmered nearby as well, as they skirted its northern end. Sometimes Sam stared off into the distance and felt strange and out of place there astride a tall horse deep in prairie grass. He could ride well enough now, after spending hours in the saddle, but something else was foreign to him here, though he couldn't track it down. The moments of detachment were fleeting, as well.

At their first campsite that evening, Sam wrapped himself in his blanket on the ground and tried to huddle close to the fire. Although no one used tobacco, Miller, Crenshaw, and their companions fortified themselves with hot coffee every evening. The aroma of it was a pleasant thing, but Bishop Rone and the boys politely declined every offer of a cup. "I got a son on a mission and a ward that expects me to live by what I preach, so I'll have to pass," said Chadester in a friendly manner.

"Seems like a little thing, Bishop, to make an issue of," said Crenshaw one night at the fire. "My family's Mormon. We all are. Hot coffee on a cold prairie is what got the pioneers to Utah, if you don't mind my sayin' so."

"I don't mind," said Chadester.

"I'm out here, risking life and limb, lookin' for a killer," continued Crenshaw. "The Lord ain't gonna hold no cup of coffee against me, as far as I can see."

"Coffee? No, I wouldn't think so."

The lawman shrugged. "What's the point of it all, then? This ain't whiskey we're talkin' about. It's a simple thing. You and your boys could use a cup of coffee in this weather. Your missionary son ain't here. Your ward members ain't here. Besides, I don't think none of 'em would really care."

The six men around the fire sat listening to Crenshaw, a large, dark-haired fellow with sharp features. The glow of the flames reflected in their faces. Some of them sipped their coffee as they waited for Chadester to respond. "John and Sam, here, are welcome to the coffee if they want it," Bishop Rone began. "They're grown men, as you are, and can choose one way or another for themselves."

"Hah!" laughed Crenshaw, elbowing John next to him. "Not with the old man watchin'." John gave him a friendly push-back for his trouble.

"The issue here isn't really coffee, boys," said Bishop Rone. "Why, the day may come when the Church decides there's no harm in it, or at least not enough to make a difference, but right now, at this point in time, they've asked us to refrain. It would be better for us if we did refrain; it would please the Lord if we did. Now, I don't know why that's so. I don't believe the Lord will be *too* angry with us if we can't. Habit and culture are powerful things. Sometimes even righteousness takes a generation or so to ease into. No, I don't believe it's really about coffee. It's more about edging us along toward a better life. It's one minor step I've pledged to take. You boys can do as you please, but I reckon I'll keep that pledge for now."

Crenshaw and Miller and the others were just as friendly to Sam and the Chadesters as they ever were, and they still drank their coffee, but not as often and not as much, and it was interesting to Sam that they didn't really seem to mind or make it an issue anymore.

It was late September, and the summer sun still burned at noon, but at night the air turned crisp and cold. The riders could measure the temperature drop with every mile covered from midday until dusk, and patches of clouds near the hills made the trail as gloomy as a shadow by five o'clock.

John and Sam were beginning to suspect the futility of the journey, but finally a couple named Butcher at an isolated house twenty miles south of Cedar Fort told them they'd seen a lone rider moving west through the sage two days before on a big bay horse.

"I never approached 'im," said the farmer, "and he stayed some distance away, but he could be the fella you're lookin' for. I know most of the local folks, and he wasn't one of them."

That news pointed the posse in a particular direction. Not too long after that, Miller found some horseshoe tracks that had the X imprint, and the men were further encouraged.

"We're getting warmer, boys," said Crenshaw and led out eagerly until the once-promising trail finally dissolved into thistle weed and dust.

"Let's spread out in a line about five yards apart," ordered Miller. "Try to pick up that shoe print again, and yell out to the others if you do."

When the lawmen moved away, John sidled up to his father and complained, "The wind's likely blown any prints into sand by now, Pa. We ought to ride up in those ridges yonder and see if we can spy old Sullivan on the other side."

"Miller's the man in charge here, John. You let him do what he thinks best. We're guests here. Don't you go steppin' on any toes."

"I'm thinkin' we could probably see Sullivan from those ridges, if he's out here anywhere."

"Could be, but Miller will come to that notion soon enough. Unless he asks our counsel, it's better not to offer it."

The sky loomed large above the riders, fanned out as they were, and soon Miller, a detective more accustomed to working in the confines of Provo and Salt Lake, ran his eye along the higher ridges to the west. "The hoof prints seemed to have vanished," he noted, riding up alongside Chadester. "I say we comb those ridges over there and then send one fellow up high to take a look over the valley on the other side. Maybe he could catch a glimpse of something."

"Good idea." The bishop nodded. "I'll tell my boys, and we'll head that way." Chadester winked at John when he caught up with him. "Let's go follow orders," he called, and the horses were off and running.

The rocks and boulders below the ridgeline were rough and cracked and difficult to climb. Old silver mines and tunnels littered the area and were well known to local men. "Many a grizzled desert rat has wasted to dry bones trapped and entombed in the worst of these," the bishop told John and Sam, although he said nothing to Miller and the others. "I used to come out here in the early days with your granddad. There were beastly critters then, as there are now, and they usually ended up in some dark hole." The posse tethered their horses in a shallow clearing beneath some cedar trees and explored the immediate area, guns and rifles at the ready.

Then Miller directed Sam and John to scale a route to the top of the highest ridge. "Work your way around the rocks. Don't try to go straight up. It may take you a while, but you've got a few hours yet 'fore dark."

With canteens strapped to their shoulders, the two friends hurried off, Sam letting John take the lead. It reminded him of the day some weeks before when they pushed the Saxon together, and after that when they worked the hay, getting sunburned side by side. Now they were climbing a mountain, struggling, working to bring justice to George Sullivan, once again working for an objective, for something good.

After an hour of inching upward between the boulders and pulling themselves through narrow gullies and pathways of cracked stone, they reached a rocky summit and looked out across the flatlands from whence they'd come. They could see the Butcher place, the house of the rancher who'd directed them, far in the shimmering distance like a discarded toy. They could even see the Wasatch Range in the east and the glint of civilization underneath it. In the west they could see more prairie and a hundred miles of wilderness to search. But they could not see Mick Sullivan or the big bay he was supposedly riding with the telltale X on his iron shoes.

John found a smooth, flat boulder and sat on it awhile, looking out across the vista as he chewed on a long piece of grass. Sam joined him there, not anxious to start down. The wind blew his hair and billowed his shirt, and he welcomed the cool relief. "Wild goose chase, huh?" he muttered to John and was surprised at his friend's response.

"Naw, I don't look at it that way," he said. "Sure, I want to find Mick, but trying has been worth something. Seeing this prairie again has been worth something. The journey, Sam, that's been worth something too." He spit out the weed and eyed the horizon again. "Life's like that. It's just hard to see sometimes."

Rifle shots suddenly cracked out below, and John and Sam were jolted back to reality. They scrambled down the rocks, scraping, sliding, wrestling with every tangle of brush, every snagging branch, every miserable stone. More shots pierced the gathering shadows and echoed from a ragged wall of granite to the south. John and Sam retreated from the sound and finally came upon their companions by crawling through a slot trail at the other end of the clearing from where they'd left them.

"Pa, are you all right?" John yelled as he saw his father. "Is it Sullivan?"

Bishop Rone grabbed both young men in his arms. "Thank God," he said. He was crouched down, as were the others, against a barricade of logs and stones. Miller and Crenshaw had their rifles trained at some spot on the cliffs above, and the other deputy was bent over a wounded man who was writhing on a blanket in the grass.

"It's Sullivan, all right," said Chadester. "He called out to us before he started shooting, spitting all kinds of filth. Said we couldn't take him. Then he opened up on us. Poor Chambers here took one in the thigh. He's gonna need a doctor." The three of them moved closer to the wounded deputy. His bleeding upper leg had been wrapped and tied with a tourniquet. He was groaning, and his face was pale.

Crenshaw fired twice more with his rifle, and another shot echoed in return. All of them squinted in the direction of the sound and then looked back anxiously at Chambers. Bishop Chadester knelt beside him. He pressed water to his lips. John joined him there, looking solemnly at the terrible wound that had ravaged the deputy's leg.

Miller was growing impatient behind the barricade. Several seconds passed with Sullivan staying silent, not returning fire. The men waited, watching nervously, listening for any movement from above. Crenshaw tried to draw the fugitive out again by sending a couple of rounds toward the cliffs. There was no response. Miller slid over from the barricade. "Sullivan's out of ammunition. That gun he stole was loaded, but he had nothing extra. I figure that's why he's stopped shootin'. Crenshaw, Gill, and me are gonna sneak up the back of that ridgeline over there and take him from the other side. It'll be dark soon, so we can't wait no longer. We can use your boys and their flashlights. The more men we have, the sooner we'll find 'im. You stay here with Chambers till we get back."

"I'll stay with Chambers," said Moroni Chadester, "but I'm sending John and Sam to that farmhouse for a wagon. It'll take you fellas all night to find Mick Sullivan, *if* you find him, and this man needs a doctor. We've got to get him back to town."

Miller considered this. "Well, I'll take their weapons then," he said. "I need every gun I have against this fella, and I'll need the flashlights too."

Chadester was adamant. "I'm not sending my boys off in the dark without flashlights or sidearms."

"Look here," said Miller. "I've got a job to do. Catching that fugitive comes first. I brought you along as a courtesy, Bishop, but I'm the one in charge here. I'm the one who says how things are gonna be."

"The flashlights are mine," said Chadester, "and so are these two young fellas kneeling there, when it comes to things that count."

Sam watched as Crenshaw and the other deputy waited nervously. Miller was not an overbearing boss, but he was a proud man and didn't like being second-guessed. He looked at Chadester, unwilling to back down. "I'm requiring you by law to turn over them flashlights," he demanded. "I'm doing it as the commanding officer here."

"You're right, you are in charge." Chadester spoke yet with a forcefulness that gave Sam pause. "But you have a badly injured man here who needs a doctor. He may lose his leg or his life without one. *He's* your first priority, this man who needs your help. My boys and I intend to get him help as quickly as we can, and we need to keep our guns and flashlights to safely do it. You also have a wanted man somewhere on that mountain, but he's secondary now. You can go looking for him in the dark, if that's what you want to do. You won't find him. I can tell you that much, even as we're hiding here. My guess is, he's long gone because he's out of shells and out of daylight, so he's got no reason to hang around." Bishop Rone's eyes met Miller's as he finished, spitting his words. "Now, John and Sam are riding off for Butcher's place, and they're taking their guns and their flashlights with them. I'm staying here with Chambers till they get back. What you fellas do is up to you."

Miller was suddenly furious. He moved to meet Chadester eye to eye, his jawline stiff and tight. "Maybe you're doin' this for Chambers, Bishop, but maybe you got other reasons too. Sullivan was a friend of yours. He was in your ward. Maybe you're ashamed of how you folks protected him or were blinded to what he'd done. Maybe you'd just as soon he got away."

"That's crazy, Miller!" John spoke sharply, stepping up.

"But more than likely, you don't want your own boy, here, in danger," Miller pressed. "You don't want him going with me after Sullivan and maybe gettin' shot!"

John leaped toward Miller, about to strike him, when his father intervened. Sam jumped in to add his weight and hold John back. John was breathing hard and fighting to get free, as angry as Sam had ever seen him.

"Let me make this clear," said Chadester, looking squarely at the officer. "Mick Sullivan is no friend of mine. He murdered those who were. I live for the day when he'll be brought to justice. My son joined this posse and accepted any danger it involved because he feels the same. But tonight we have to make a choice. We can keep lookin' for Mick in the dark, or we can try to save this man."

Miller's chin dropped. He was subdued by Chadester's words. He withered under the force of them. The bishop hadn't spoken sharply or with bitterness but with a tone that left no doubt where he stood. Miller shrugged, finally, and stepped away. Sam let go of John, feeling him relax, and they both hurried to depart for the Butchers'.

Miller scowled at them over his shoulder. "The fellas and me are still goin' out, with or without your boys and their flashlights. I'm a stubborn man, and Sullivan's fightin' the dark just like we are."

"Good luck," said Chadester wearily. "If you don't mind, I'm gonna build a fire. It'll keep me and Chambers warm and help you fellas find your way back here, with or without that scum you're chasin' blind."

* * *

All of the men arrived back at the site just after dawn. Miller and his deputies were empty-handed, having spent the night in a cold cave they'd wandered into, with no safe way out until morning, once a wrong turn caused them to get lost. "Sullivan was in there at one time," claimed Miller, trying to justify himself. "We found a few matches and could see enough to know there was a camp site. Horse droppings, too, below the cliffs. He might still have that bay."

By that time, Sam and the Chadesters were busy loading Chambers in the wagon. The boys had brought blankets and fresh bandages from the Butcher place. Mr. Butcher had promised to ride into Lehi and summon an ambulance. With a surgeon and a specialist waiting at the nearest medical facility, Chambers had a better chance of keeping his leg—and even just surviving.

Bishop Rone had blessed him during the night and prayed for him and felt good about the outcome. He tied his horse to the wagon and drove the wounded deputy back across the prairie, while the others came on their own. The bishop ruffled the wounded man's hair and turned him over to the doctors, having formed a new bond with the young man. Rone promised to visit as soon as he was able.

Bob Chambers gratefully acknowledged the assistance. "You stayed awake all night with me," he whispered and only reluctantly let go of the bishop's hand once the doctors took him away.

Miller was still frustrated about losing Mick when they had come so close. "More manpower and a few lights would have nabbed him for us," he fumed. "We had him cornered, and he was out of shells. Now he's disappeared again, and who knows where he'll turn up next? We had a good chance and we lost it, and that's all I got to say."

As the bishop had comforted John over Lester Hawkins's death, now John talked to his father. "You did the right thing, Pa, no matter what Miller says. You gave him a mile of rope as the man in charge, but when it came down to it, you had to save Bob Chambers. We'll get Sullivan some other day."

"I hope so, son."

"Well, I've got no doubt about it."

Chadester answered sadly, "Often when a slippery fugitive is finally captured, it's because he's committed another crime. I pray with all my heart that's not what happens here. If we could have had Mick, and he got away, will another victim have to pay because of the choice I made? I'll live in fear of that until he's caught."

"We might never know," said John. "He'll never come back to Alpine or anywhere around here, that's for sure."

"Oh, I think he will someday," said Bishop Rone. "For some strange reason, people, even bad people, are drawn back to familiar places. They're drawn home. It may take a while. It may take years. But eventually they show up again."

Sam didn't believe it. Mick Sullivan was in the wind, and if he had any sense about him at all, he'd jump a freight train to San Francisco and anonymously work the California ranches. That's what a wanted man would do. Sam also prayed that he and the Chadesters had heard the last of Sullivan. If his eventual capture meant that he'd hurt someone else, Sam didn't want to know, if only for the sake of good Bishop Chadester, who worried over it.

*　　*　　*

Still, Sam knew, as long as a fugitive is on the loose, people are haunted by him. Even as they grew busy with other things that fall, as red and yellow leaves blossomed in the canyons and a crisp frost jeweled the higher ridges above Alpine, the ranchers and ward members still looked over their shoulders and kept watch. The fields turned flat and dun-colored, and the trees that guarded them began to sag, their leaves all wasted. If Mick

Sullivan had taken to the hills, folks said, the winter winds would soon drive him to the warmth of hearth and fire once again, though no one saw him anywhere as the days grew colder.

Carrie Warren, a friend of Laney's, got a scare when she thought she glimpsed a man who looked like Sullivan staring through the window pane late one night at the Bonney House, a restaurant where she worked in American Fork, but the fellow turned out to be Mr. Bonney's uncle from Cedar City, just trying to see if the place was still open. The uncle did look a bit like Sullivan, everyone agreed, especially through a cold window pane in reflected light, and no one blamed poor Carrie for being nervous.

Even Laney thought she saw Mick Sullivan once in Provo. She and Sam had taken a transit coach with John to the Utah County fair. John's girl, Alice Cahill, got on in Pleasant Grove, and the four of them made a day of it, visiting every livestock exhibition, pie-eating contest, juggling act, and sideshow, coming home with enough trinkets and prizes to fill a cedar chest.

It was just twilight when Laney suddenly pulled on Sam's arm. "I think I saw Mick Sullivan," she told him breathlessly.

"Where?" Sam had just won a baseball at a pitch-and-toss concession, and he immediately shoved it in his pocket. "Where? Where'd you see him?"

"Over there. He's gone now, but I'm sure it was him." Laney hesitated. "At least, I'm pretty sure." Sam questioned her further. She couldn't tell for sure. The man was in the fringe of the passing crowd, just one of many. But something separated him in her mind, she told Sam. The hunch of the shoulder? The crumpled hat over his brow? The light beard on the gaunt cheekbones? The man was looking at her, she said, and she quickly turned her eyes, as was her instinct when strangers stared, but she wished she'd kept watching, for when she looked again, he'd disappeared.

Sam turned her around to face him squarely, put his hands on her shoulders, and looked down into her eyes. "You're not seeing things in shadows, are you?" he said. "You're not afraid?"

"No." She wasn't, and she wanted him to know it. "I do wish they could catch Mick Sullivan," she said, "if only for Johnny's sake. He feels so bad about what happened, and for his father too."

Up ahead, they could see John and Alice walking together, a teasing young couple having fun. The sounds around them were full of carnival music, and the air smelled of popcorn and taffy twists. Sam knew Laney wanted to join them, to forget Mick Sullivan, to be carefree again like John and Alice. When she quickly pushed him forward so they could catch up, he understood why.

"Now I don't mind that you auctioned off that car you always bragged about," Miss Cahill was saying, "but it is a nuisance to take the transit home. There's nowhere to cuddle on a transit, if you catch my drift." She giggled, swinging the gold chain of her feathered purse on her pretty fingers.

"Yeah, it's a cryin' shame," said John, putting his arm around her as they jauntily moved along. "I guess we'll have to just make do."

Sam winked at Laney, overhearing the conversation. "Hey, listen to those two! I thought we were the ones who needed a chaperone!"

*   *   *

To try to take their minds off Mick Sullivan and every other worry, Sam and Johnny arranged with a motor coach service for a day in Salt Lake City. They and their dates could ride a train from American Fork to the Rio Grande station on the west side of downtown and be within walking distance of Temple Square, the Hotel Utah, the Beehive House, ZCMI, and a dozen restaurants, theaters, and museums. The return trip would put them back in Alpine just after dark.

With Pleasant Grove slightly inconvenient, John opted for Carrie Warren as his date, which pleased Laney, since the girls were great friends, but also because Carrie was more demure and less aggressive toward John than Alice Cahill was, a habit in Miss Cahill that Laney hadn't liked.

"She's all over Johnny," she complained to Sam once, out of earshot of the others. "She needs to let him be."

"Don't you think John leads her on?" was Sam's reply. "Don't you think he likes it when she flirts with him?"

"Well, he shouldn't," Laney retorted crisply. "And he wouldn't, if Alice would mind her manners."

Sam thought he detected a tiny spark of jealousy in Laney's tone.

She had no problem with Carrie, and the Salt Lake trip was a glittering success. The men wore dapper, flat-brimmed hats and single-breasted, tailored coats of the latest style. Meg Chadester had ordered the jackets wholesale for the store, specifically for missionaries, so they were already on hand.

The girls were outfitted in slim woolen skirts and stylish tunics and pretty hats accented with feathers in the bands, adding a new sophistication to Laney's honey-colored hair and Carrie's winsome curls.

They practically skipped their way up South Temple Street, once the train had dropped them at the station. Salt Lake wasn't new to John, but Laney and Carrie were awestruck by the tree-lined avenues, the trolley tracks, the bustling traffic rushing by. Soon the great temple ascended in front of them with its spires and its golden angel. The girls stood entranced, taking in its majestic splendor.

"Sometimes you can even catch a glimpse of the prophet strolling through the grounds," John told them. "It's not unusual at all."

"Joseph F. Smith?" said Carrie, thrilled.

"He'll be the one with the longest beard," quipped Sam, adding to the fun.

Sam wasn't quite sure how he felt about being in Salt Lake City, now that he was there. He had looked forward to the excursion since John first suggested it, and it wasn't that he felt let down or disappointed. Anywhere with Laney was heaven in his eyes. But as he looked at the familiar places once again—the temple and the tabernacle; Main Street, with its hotels and shops; State Street stretching long and straight to the southernmost points of the city—a queasiness came over him. He had seen this all before, at a different time and in a different way, and he couldn't quite determine when or how.

"Look way down there," John instructed the girls as they stood at the top of the street, just below the site where the new state capitol was being constructed. "Way down there is Sandy, the little farming area where Sam is from."

Carrie and Laney squinted into the distance and smiled at Sam.

"We gotta go down there someday and see why they had to chase him out of town," teased John, "and why no one's ever come lookin' for 'im."

"Why *is* that, Sam?" Carrie joined in the teasing.

Sam was suddenly confused and a little embarrassed. "I don't . . . I don't remember."

"It's all right, Sam," said Laney, coming quickly to the rescue. "You don't belong to Sandy anymore. You're an Alpine boy now. You belong to me. You belong to us."

Still, with this strange, yet familiar, city suddenly around him, Sam wavered. What was this queasy sensation he was experiencing, this mix of colors? They had come here at least partially to rid themselves of fear over a fugitive, and yet there were times when he seemed to be a fugitive himself, running from some unknown distant past.

In every other way, the trip could not have been more perfect. Sam laughed as Laney tried on hats at ZCMI. The four of them ate at Clancy's Café on the corner of Main Street and 100 South. They found an outdoor concert under a bowery near the Eagle Gate, the fall weather still being fine enough to allow it, and they even danced around a sidewalk organ grinder and threw an exorbitant number of pennies in his cup. All went well, but still Sam fidgeted. The day was glorious, but he was glad enough when the time came to be back on the train, with Laney's golden head against his shoulder, heading back to Alpine and the world he had come to know. He was an Alpine boy and thanked God for it. He was glad to be going home.

Christmas Winds

December 4, 1915—Since our troubles, the Lord remembered us and blessed us with a lovely fall. Now the cold is clamping down as full-blown winter approaches. My little flock is well, with Sister Sullivan and the children my greatest concern, along with the Williams boy. He has such a lively little spirit, and his family loves him so. Pray God he lasts through Christmas. We don't need another Tiny Tim in this town, with no repentant Scrooge to come to his assistance. I'm only a bishop and must abide by the Father's will.

Moroni Chadester Journal

Chapter Nine

IN DECEMBER, LANEY WILLIAMS TOOK a part-time job at the mercantile store Bishop Chadester owned in town, both to help with the holiday rush and to bolster her own family's income. Doctor Billingham's visits were becoming more frequent, as Joey seemed to have developed some kind of respiratory infection and was coughing almost continually. Sam was constantly pressed by an urge to take the boy to Salt Lake City and find a specialist there, but he had no authority in the matter, and Billingham assured Kit and Johanna that he was doing all that could be done. His syrups would eventually kill the infection, if the boy was kept warm and vaporous salves were applied. About the middle of the month Joey seemed to rally, and the Williams family breathed more easily as he did.

At the store Laney found a wonderful set of Indian beads some manufacturer in Denver had put together, claiming it was of "genuine Paiute" origin.

"Look," she showed Sam. "There are enough beads here to make a concho belt. I'm buying it for Joey. His legs may not work, but his fingers do. Why, he'll love creating something beautiful with his own hands!" She packed up the supplies, which included the multicolored beads, the leather backing and strings, the needle and thread, and several decorative pieces to enhance the final product. Laney was thrilled, imagining what Joey might accomplish. "He's an artist, I tell you. Everyone thinks that because he can't speak, he doesn't recognize great beauty, but he does."

"Oh, I can tell that," Sam agreed. He was picking Laney up after work in the Williamses' car. He quickly took her packages as she buttoned up against the cold. "He recognizes *you*, doesn't he?"

Smiling, she tweaked his chin to thank him for the compliment.

"Besides," added Sam, "who says Joey never speaks? I've heard him say one word, and if he never says another, his language is complete. 'Laney.' He loves you as I do, so it's the only word with any meaning for either of us." With that, he bent and kissed her as she was about to step into the car. He would have lingered there in her arms forever if she had let him, but the homeward road beckoned, and Laney was anxious for Joey to see the beads.

"You're not going to wait for Christmas?" said Sam, shifting the gears beside her.

"No, I don't think so. I think Joey will want to get started right away . . . while he's feeling well enough." There was an ache in Laney's tone, and she dropped her eyes.

Sam reached across and took her hand. "Yes, that's best," he said. "He can finish it and hang it on the tree for Christmas."

That night they sat around the Williamses' kitchen table, and Laney spread her purchase before her brother. His eyes grew wide at the multicolored beads, the leather, and the available patterns for design—the lines and squares and circles, the flames and feathers, each shape his for the choosing. Laney let him know that he was the master here. The belt was his to create, to mold and shape as he desired. Carefully, she showed him how to thread the needle through the tiny beads, anchoring each one firmly in its place. She let him choose a pattern and then demonstrated how to follow it, completing a single strip herself. All the while, he eyed her lovingly, and when at last she took his hands and guided his fingers through the motions with her own, he squealed and clamored with delight.

Soon he was working on his own, looking to Laney for approval, but sewing together with his own hands the beads that would form the belt. The colors of the beads drew Sam's attention. Red, blue, green, purple, gold— so vivid they seemed to pulsate for a moment, causing him to blink. Then Joey's shrill excitement overwhelmed the onlookers, and everyone turned their eyes to his fingers, moving rapidly through the paces. He preferred blue and purple above the other colors and used them even when changes were suggested. His work was often crooked and he had trouble following the pattern precisely, but Laney let him be.

"Crooked is creative," she said more than once as she encouraged the boy along. "True art is seldom perfect in line and square and measure."

Watching from the chair next to Sam, Kit Williams sipped his Brigham tea. "God works miracles in that boy," he whispered, "and He works 'em best through Laney. She's always had a way with him. It's a gift she has, ya know."

"I *do* know, Brother Williams," murmured Sam. "I surely do."

Sister Williams—Johanna—nodded as she too quietly watched Joey and Laney work. Her eyes were shining. Like Laney, she was a beautiful woman, with thick, lustrous hair and smooth skin. But sorrow over her lost children had taken its toll, and she was no longer the young soul that Laney was now, eager and full of life. Sam looked at the mother and hoped the daughter would never have to suffer as Johanna had. He sometimes thought that Sister Williams was as fragile as a reed, and one more loss would be more than she could ever survive. But Laney disagreed.

"My mother is stronger than you think," she said later, as they lingered on the porch. "She's resigned to Joey's eventual passing, as we all are. It will break her heart, but she will thank God she had him for as long as she did, considering every year a blessing." Wrapped in a woolen scarf and cap against the cold, Laney stood with rosy cheeks and winter breath and a reluctance to say good-bye, in spite of the frosty air. Her blonde hair framed her face, and her braid fell over the shoulder of her coat. Sam hung on her every word. "My mother wanted children so desperately," she said. "Each loss was devastating, but it also steeled her. She'll suffer when Joey goes, but she'll know how to survive."

"And she'll still have you." Sam smiled, changing the tone and drawing her to him. "At least until I take you away."

"Now, that just might kill her!" teased Laney, kissing him with an eagerness that he was more than willing to return.

*   *   *

"Can I talk to you, sir?" Sam stood at the door of Bishop Chadester's study, a varnished room of bookcases surrounding a large oak desk. There were papers and binders everywhere: business files, ranch summaries, church reports, journals. The bishop looked up, still cheerful in the face of it.

"Come on in," he said, with a wave of his hand. "You're a welcome sight, with all of this before me!"

Sam had knocked softly, knowing that private moments for Rone Chadester were precious, but the man's smile was genuine. He was garrulous and accommodating as always, rising from his chair and offering his time.

"Just a word, sir," Sam repeated, "if you don't mind."

"Why, of course, my boy! As a matter of fact, I've been hoping to catch a moment or two with you myself." He came around the desk to put his hand on Sam's shoulder and direct him to a comfortable chair. "I've been meaning to thank you in particular for joining John and me out there on the prairie when we was lookin' for Mick Sullivan. That was risky, and no matter what you say, you didn't have to come."

"I'm glad I was there."

Chadester sat down again, plaintively rubbing his chin as he eyed Sam across the desk. He finally spoke, his tone fatherly and gentle. "You've been a wonderful addition to this household, Sam, to say nothing of what you've done for Johnny. He had a hard time of it when Andy left. You've become a brother to him and filled that void." The bishop paused and eyed Sam tentatively. "What would you think if I told you that I prayed you here? What would you think of that?" Chadester's eyes twinkled as he settled back in his chair. "Yes, I prayed you here, and the good Lord answered, for John's sake."

"And my own," returned Sam graciously.

"I've never really asked you much about your family or where you came from," said Chadester. "I figured that was your business and if you wanted to tell me, you would. John vouched for you, and that was good enough. Your work and behavior since you came have proved him right. You're a fixture around here now, and you can stay as long as you like; although, if you have a mother and father somewhere, you ought to let them know. Families matter, Sam, even when a boy grows up."

"I have a family somewhere," Sam began. "At least, I think I do. Would you believe me if I said I don't remember? I must have hit my head or something because blurry images sometimes come and go, and everything seems so far away. It's strange. I'm okay. I feel fine. It's just that there's some part of the past that won't come into focus." Sam hesitated. He wasn't here to talk about a family he didn't remember. "Anyway, it'll all come back to me one of these days, and I'll rush home to Mama. In the meantime, I guess I need some fatherly advice."

"Fatherly advice, is it?" Bishop Chadester laughed. "Well, I guess that's what I'm best at."

"Even though you're John's father, not mine?"

Chadester cleared his throat. Sam guessed that his past was an intriguing puzzle to this kind man, who wasn't quite ready to let the subject go. He even sensed that Chadester wanted to ask him more personal questions.

Had he been abused or abandoned? Perhaps his neurological forgetfulness was a mechanism of escape. The truth was, Sam didn't know. He only trusted what he felt. Chadester seemed to love him like a son and was perfectly willing to be his surrogate father. As for advice, that was the man's specialty.

"Son, I know as well as any father what you're gonna ask," he said, "and I can probably give you a straighter answer because I know the girl involved."

As nervous as he was, Sam didn't know whether this was a good way to start or not; he had failed to see the gleam in Bishop Chadester's eye. "How did you . . . I mean, you know what I'm here to talk about?"

"Well," answered Chadester, "it's plain to see that you've fallen like a sawed-off timber for Laney Williams. I assume that's why you're here."

"Yes, sir." Sam's emotions suddenly spilled forward. "I can't begin to tell you how much I love her. I can't begin to tell you how I feel."

"No need. I understand."

"I don't. I don't understand at all. I've kissed and teased and played and flirted with other girls, but I've never experienced anything like this. It's more than I ever expected, and I don't quite know what to do about it. I want to do the right thing . . . for Laney . . . but I'm not sure I can . . ."

The bishop suddenly stiffened. "I told you once to mind your manners with that girl," he said sternly. "I hope you've done that. I hope you haven't taken advantage of her in any way."

"No, of course not." Sam shuddered, instantly regretting he'd ever walked into the room.

"Kit Williams owns a .30/.30, and he's not afraid to use it," Chadester growled. "Why, he scattered buckshot clear to Lehi once, chasing some drummer from Salt Lake who was passing through and took a shine to Laney."

"A drummer?" Sam gulped.

"You know, one of those traveling salesmen. That fella's still picking BBs out of his britches, is my guess." The bishop shuffled some papers on his desk as he caught his breath. "You got any confessions you want to make to me, Brother Carroll, so I can try to figure what to do about Kit Williams and his gun?"

For a full minute, Chadester's face looked as gray as thunder. His brow was creased, his expression stern and tight.

Sam fidgeted in his chair. "Confessions?"

"That's what I said. Confessions."

"A few unworthy thoughts, maybe," Sam stuttered. "Some urges I'm ashamed of—but never acted on . . . because . . . well, because I wouldn't do that to Laney. I care about her, and I want to be as good as she thinks I am, so I can honestly say I showed restraint. Though, there were those thoughts I mentioned."

"Yes, those thoughts." The bishop scowled.

Sam's knees were turning to water. He didn't know what to make of this "fatherly" confidante whom he had come to trust. Then, just as suddenly, the frown lifted. Chadester smiled, and his eyes brightened. Seeing fear in Sam's face, he even laughed a little.

"I'm a bishop, boy. I have to act like one, on occasion."

"Yes, sir." Sam ventured a grin, relieved at the change in tone but still wary about what was coming next.

"I was a young man once myself, and I know how these things go," laughed Chadester. "I know how you feel toward Laney. I know your desires, Sam. Our natural inclinations shouldn't be a source of guilt. They have their purposes. Still, in this area, the Lord has set the standard high, most likely 'cause he loves us." The bishop paused, noting Sam's uncomfortably downcast eyes. "Do you remember that night on the prairie?" he asked. "When Crenshaw and the others were ribbing me about the coffee?"

Sam nodded, not seeing the connection.

"Crenshaw said he thought the good Lord would forgive a coffee drinker on his way to catch a killer, or words to that effect, and I agreed. There's no comparing the two transgressions, killing and coffee drinking. But I tried to make the point that by passing up on coffee, or any minor thing like that, I was simply trying to raise the bar a little bit, do one more thing the Lord's asked me to do. I'm not a bad man if I fail, but I'm a better man if I don't."

Chadester pushed himself away from his desk. He looked across at Sam with more understanding and fatherly affection than the young man had ever seen or felt. It was almost as if God himself were sitting there, counseling His son. Not a wayward son, but an average son, a normal son.

"So you love the girl?" said Chadester finally.

"More than I ever thought I could," Sam answered.

"I hear that all the time, you know."

"But I do. I really do."

"Of course you do. What young man wouldn't?"

"There's more to it than that."

"Seems to me we better plan a wedding, then." The bishop smiled. "That is, if Laney and her parents are favorable to the idea."

"But I have no career, sir, no way to support a wife."

"A tall, strapping fella like you? That should be no problem," said Chadester. "Work for me until you can make your own way. That's how it's done. Us older folks help the younger ones along."

Sam was still hesitant. Something inside him resisted Chadester's solution. Sam really didn't know who he was or where he'd come from, but being chained to the daily grind of the everyday world was not how he had imagined spending his youth. He was sure of that. It wasn't that he didn't want to marry Laney—he loved her beyond reason. It was surrendering himself to conformity. That's what bothered him. It went against his grain.

"You're reluctant to be tied down, aren't you?" mused the bishop, as if he were reading Sam's mind. "You think marriage will mean the end of something, and it will. It will mean the end of living only for yourself."

"I live for Laney now," said Sam defensively.

"Only as it pleases you," answered Chadester. "Once you're married, what pleases *her* must take precedence, as your needs will for her. That's what love is. That's the plan. It's how God made us. It's not easy, a commitment like that. There are lots of challenges. That's why the attraction between two people is so powerful, I guess. We mortals wouldn't make the leap on the strength of love alone. Nature has to get involved as well."

"I used to be more than satisfied with the 'nature' part," said Sam. "Real love changes things."

"It makes every other sacrifice worthwhile, Sam; every other joy pales in its shadow. Take it while you can. It's a gift that may not come again, at least not with this intensity."

Minutes later when Chadester walked him to the door and shook his hand, Sam wondered what he'd done to deserve this wise man's friendship, his fatherly affection, his kindliness.

"By the way," said Bishop Rone, as Sam was leaving, "Kit Williams doesn't really own a shotgun. He's never had to worry about Laney. Drummers come and go, but Laney has always managed things just fine, as she has with you. Women make good men better. I think she must be destiny's child, Sam, meant in the end for just one man. I'll be pleased to see that destiny come to pass."

Chapter Ten

Sam had no ring for Laney, but after he spoke to Bishop Chadester and to Kit Williams, there was a definite understanding that sometime in the spring he and Laney would wed. In the meantime, he cherished every second in her presence, especially those that they could spend alone.

He was welcomed wholeheartedly into the Williams family, and Joey became a constant companion, often clinging to his neck and shoulders as he walked about the place. Johanna Williams seemed quite content with the notion that she was "gaining a fine son," not losing a daughter—"As long as you don't take her south of Provo," she said. So it wasn't for lack of acceptance that he ached for those moments when he and Laney could have the world to themselves—in the buggy, in the back of the shop, or sometimes even under the steeple again, where they had first kissed. He loved her, and sometimes in her embrace, he felt that his soul would melt.

They both knew and remembered the laws of chastity. She knew where she was vulnerable. He knew where he must not touch her, though he wanted to. *Nature gets involved as well*, as Bishop Chadester had said. But when he was tempted to cross the line, Laney was sensitive to the moment and did her part in keeping them both in bounds.

"I believe in our future," she told him once. "I want it to be free of any regret."

"I pray for that as well," he whispered, and though it was difficult, he tried to make her definition of *regret* his own.

And so Christmas loomed for the little town in the fields beneath the mountains, and Bishop Chadester's Alpine tried to forget its recent terrors with an engagement and a joyous season, complete with the good food, good cheer, and the goodwill of neighbors who made a point of visiting each and every home in the little ward. There was the usual glitter and festivity of the holiday, some of it purchased at the mercantile but much of it handmade. Lanterns blazed above the snowy streets, trimmed with ribbons and mistletoe.

Christmas trees were cut fresh from the benches and dragged to each home behind teams of horses wearing harness bells for the occasion. "It's a tradition here," John told Sam. "When you bring your tree in, the bells signal its arrival." Those trees were soon adorned with silver angels, strings of popcorn, and candy canes. In every parlor, hot chocolate or cider was served around the fireplace while someone played the family organ and "Silent Night" was sung.

Laney welcomed Primary children to the store and, on a wide counter, made paper stars and candles with them and helped them glue on glitter and cellophane to make the ornaments shine. She let them wrap gifts there and add their creations to the packaging. Sometimes she helped customers order items from the mercantile catalogues—pocket knives, shaving razors, special tools for the men; jewelry, combs, and beauty products for the women—that had to come from Salt Lake and beyond.

"It always thrills me," she told Sam, "to see some boy count the small change he's been saving all year to buy his ma a pretty new brooch for Christmas. I get to see into people's hearts this time of year, and it always softens mine."

John packed all of his friends aboard the hay wagon one night and took them caroling in the cold. Making sure that everyone was warm and well wrapped in coats and caps and blankets, he drove the team down each snowy road and country lane in Alpine and let Sam and Laney and the others sing "Oh Come, All Ye Faithful" and "Deck the Halls" at every lighted porch they passed. The stars glowed overhead like crusted sugar, and with the harmonizing voices and Laney warm beside him, Sam was caught up in the romance of the moment. He looked at John, alone up on the wagon seat, and thought of the satisfaction that comes from seeing other people happy. John seemed to have learned that lesson some time ago.

"Hey, where's Alice from Pleasant Grove tonight?" Sam slid up on the wagon seat the next time Laney and the others were invited inside a house to have a sip of chocolate.

John smiled. "Pleasant Grove's a long way off in this weather," he said good-naturedly. "Besides, tonight I'm drivin'. I got no time for spoonin'. This team takes both hands."

"Yeah, and so would Alice, from what I've seen. I think you'd better find a girl like Carrie Warren in Alpine. They're nicer here."

"You got that right," said John, in a more serious tone than Sam expected. John looked at him squarely, and the hurt in his eyes belied his words. Suddenly a jolt of pain went through Sam's heart, almost like a knife. "Hey, don't think it matters, you and Laney. If it wasn't me, I'm glad it's you. I told you a long time ago that all me and Laney could ever be was friends. I was resigned then, and I'm resigned now. Don't be thinkin' you took anything from me."

Sam didn't think he'd taken anything, but as he slapped John's shoulder and drew back to welcome Laney and the others onto the wagon, he couldn't help wondering if John's giving heart had been too kind when it came to love.

*   *   *

The public highlight of the season was a Christmas concert and devotional held at the Alpine Stake Tabernacle in American Fork. Less than five years old, the building was a large edifice of yellow brick and stone, erected without the cupolas and steeples of earlier pioneer churches. The folks of northern Utah County were proud of it. Provo had its pretty four-turret tabernacle, and now there was another one, a different one, that Alpine Stake could call its own. On a frosty night, automobiles and wagons gathered around the block on every side. Men and women in fur hats and coats made their way up the steps to the doors and into the hall, where the pews were filling and garlands of pine boughs and red ribbons wound around the balcony above.

Accompanied by an orchestra, a fifty-member choir was already in full song on the podium as the audience arrived, and Sam recognized several familiar faces as he and Laney found seats that afforded them an excellent view of the pulpit and the stage. He held her hand and listened to the familiar hymns and carols, and they heartily joined in when the congregation was invited to lend its voice in rapture to the celebration. Never had the songs sounded so beautiful. Never had the bells of Christmas soared with such splendor and majesty. It was not the concert alone that was providing him this new appreciation for the season, nor was it the setting, a tabernacle proudly built after much sacrifice and labor. He had been to Christmas concerts before in fine surroundings. It was Laney, to be sure, holding his hand and pressing close to him, her eyes so beautiful and full of light. It was John and his friendship and goodness, and Bishop Rone, presiding over his little town, even in its terrible sorrow, with love and dignity. They had all changed Christmas for him.

"With our countless blessings these past few months," said the stake president in his address, "our area has also been struck with sorrow. Two fine brethren in Alpine met tragic ends at the hands of someone they trusted. Much like our Savior, whose birth we celebrate, a Judas in their lives betrayed that trust in the worst possible way. What happened was a terrible thing. It's left us all a little shaken in the security we've always felt here in these mountain valleys. But I tell you, Brothers and Sisters, with all my heart, you need not be shaken in your faith. The bells will ring this Christmas as they always have. The herald angels will sing. They will remind us again that because of the Christ child, because of that Holy Child in the manger and His atoning sacrifice, sin will be overcome, good men will live again, and we can ever be secure in that."

* * *

Sam noticed that every family in town made a point of visiting Eleanor Sullivan sometime in December. Kit and Johanna Williams took caramel apples and popcorn balls one night a week before Christmas, allowing Joey to pull the treasure on his scoot-sled while wrapped around Sam's back. Sister Williams brought a new baby quilt as well, and Eleanor, tremendously grateful, looked as if she'd need it before the year turned over.

"Oh, look what you've done with the stars!" cried Laney, seeing where the Sullivan girls had hung the decorations they'd made at the mercantile. "They are ten times prettier here than when I saw them last, and I loved them then!"

"Please, please, take off your coats and keep us company awhile," said Eleanor. "I have some wassail on the stove."

"Yes, and it smells wonderful too," Johanna told her. "It's Christmas clear to the gatepost with that aroma floatin' by."

Sam sat down next to Tommy Sullivan and asked if he remembered pitching hay in the summer sun and if the blisters he got from doing it had healed. "They'll pop up again when you shovel snow," he said, "but you can be proud of 'em. Blisters and calluses are signs of a working man's hands, and there's nothing wrong with that."

Laney and her mother spent time chatting with Eleanor. Kit Williams and Sam attempted to draw Tommy from his adolescent shell. But most of everyone's attention was centered on Joey and the little girls, especially Annabelle, the seven-year-old, who delighted in pushing him about on his sled and tossing popcorn in his mouth to make him laugh. A pretty child, with long golden ringlets and a cherubic smile, Annabelle took pleasure in showing Joey how to dance from the waist up, holding each of his hands and swinging his arms to the rhythm of several high-spirited tunes she knew, leaving both of them giggling once the frolic had ended.

"I love you, Joey!" she cried, as the evening drew to a close and the Williams family packed up to leave. Annabelle bent and pressed her cheek next to Joey's and put a Christmas ornament in his hand, a glass donkey, which she said should belong to him "because you don't have to walk when you've got a good donkey to ride." She kissed him on the cheek, and everyone laughed and clapped, and Joey beamed. During the nights that followed, Joey clutched the donkey on his pillow as he slept and insisted that it always remain within his reach.

His other prized possession, the beaded concho belt, had been hung high on the Christmas tree, and Laney assumed that's where the glass donkey would go, but Joey made it clear that the donkey was his to touch at all times, and he needed it to be where that was possible. Often he would stare in wonder at the little object, running his fingers over its molded form and smiling as he held its transparent body up to the light. Then he would sit and ponder, locked in his own mysterious state, until one morning, Laney jubilantly told Sam, with a sudden shriek of gladness he came joyfully scooting into the parlor.

"Laney! Laney! Laney!" The only word he knew leaped from Joey's throat, and his arms extended in eagerness toward the top of the Christmas tree, where the concho belt hung in all its beaded glory. From his sled, Joey reached and strained and groaned and called his sister's name. When she came running, it was plain to see what he wanted.

"I wish you could have seen his face," she laughed to Sam, continuing the story.

The beaded concho belt was far from perfect. The colors were garish and mismatched. Joey'd had trouble following the pattern and staying exactly within the prescribed lines. The Indian pyramids looked more like crooked stairs, the eagle's wings like sparrow tails. But from his father's arms Joey had placed the belt at the top of the tree with all the pride of the finest artist and had treasured his creation beyond words.

Now he wanted to take it down.

Laney retrieved the belt and hung it around his neck. "It looks pretty here too," she said, patting his cheek. "Is this where you want it, where you can touch it, like the donkey?"

Immediately, Joey slid toward the closet door, pulling it open to reach for his cap and coat. Dragging them behind him, he wheeled back into the parlor, passing his mother at the piano and his father stoking the fire, determined to reach the porch before anyone could change his plans. Laney stopped him, jumping between his sled and the front door and dropping to her knees with smiles and kisses. "Where do you think you're going? It's cold out there!"

"What's got into him?" said Kit Williams, eyeing the two of them.

Laney ran her fingers along the blue and purple beads of the belt around Joey's neck. "I think I know," she said.

"Well, he can't go out today," said Johanna, "at least not alone. A person could freeze even sitting on the porch."

Laney looked into Joey's eyes and saw a familiar light. "Sam's coming over later," she told her parents. "We'll take him for a ride and keep him warm."

"I suppose he's a better chaperone than none." Kit winked, returning to his fire.

She sat on the floor and spoke quietly with Joey, managing to settle him, as usual, with her gentle ways. She smiled when he refused to give up his coat and when he attempted more than once to drive his sled past her through the parlor door.

"You little angel," she whispered in his ear. "I know what you're thinking." Deciding there was something magical in the anonymity of Joey's plans, Laney said nothing to her parents. She was reminded of the pleasure of secret prayer or goodness behind closed doors.

When Sam came, she confided in him out of necessity, sharing the entire story. They bundled Joey in his coat and carried him through the frosty twilight to the wagon. He sat between them, buried beneath his cap, as Sam prodded the team toward the Sullivan house three miles down the road.

Then, seated on Sam's lap in front of a snapping fire in Eleanor's front parlor, Joey presented his beloved concho belt to Annabelle. Fumbling to get it off his neck, he pushed it toward her awkwardly, as if he weren't quite sure she'd want it. Sam quickly explained to Eleanor, "Joey made this, and he hopes that Annabelle will like it."

"Oh, I love it!" squealed Annabelle, pressing the beaded belt to her chest and showing it to Loretta, who danced about as if it belonged to her. "It's so beautiful!" Even Tommy moved close enough to examine the patterns on the belt and nod his detached approval.

"Of course, Joey would want all of you to enjoy it," Sam hurried to add, "and you can, if Annabelle hangs it on the tree."

"Oh, I will," cried the girl. "I'll hang it from the tallest branch, and when Christmas is over, it will go above the bed—Loretta's and mine—and we'll never forget who gave it to us either."

Through all of this, Joey clapped his hands and waved his arms in sheer delight. Laney had taken him from Sam's lap and set him on the floor, and the children gathered round and kissed him. Eleanor Sullivan, on her knees, took his cheeks between her hands. "Bless you, boy," she said. "Made with your own fingers." Suddenly she straightened and took his hand. Pressing it to her protruding stomach, she asked, "Do you feel that, Joey? Even my baby's jumpin' for joy over your goodness to our family!"

This brought laughter all around and a puzzled expression from Joey, although the light never left his eyes.

*   *   *

On Christmas Eve, Bishop and Sister Chadester and John ended their visits to ward members at the Williamses' house, where Sam was already opening presents with Laney and her family. The Chadesters brought mincemeat and pecan pies to add to the spread, and Johanna served roasted duck to all of them at a long table in the parlor. Kit Williams read aloud an abridged version of *A Christmas Carol*—with apologies to Mr. Dickens for leaving out any mention that Tiny Tim might die—and Laney added a memorized rendition of the second chapter of Luke, which Bishop Rone declared "first rate." Then they sang hymns together—all of the favorites, even the pioneer songs that had nothing to do with Christmas. "'Beautiful Zion' and 'Come, Come, Ye Saints' always remind us of home," said Bishop Rone, "and that's part of the holidays."

After Joey was put to bed with promises of a joyous Christmas morning, the adults lingered in chairs around the hearth, the light of the fire reflecting in their faces. Sam and Laney shared a leather sofa in one corner of the circle, sitting close together, arms entwined. Bishop Rone was taken by the scene. "I understand you'll have a wedding coming in the new year, Kit," he said so everyone could hear. "Are you ready to give up Laney to this stranger?"

Everyone laughed, Sam a little uncomfortably.

"He lives in your house, Bishop. He ain't no stranger to you. If you vouch for him, I guess I'll have to go along."

"Hey, you're not putting this on me," laughed Chadester in good spirit. "Your daughter, your decision."

Kit looked pensively for a moment at Laney, and Sam saw a shadow of anguish flee across his face. But he recovered quickly and answered Chadester with the same light tone. "These are modern times, Bishop. I don't reckon I have much say in the matter."

"Well, I do," declared Johanna, suddenly coming to life. "And I'm all for it! It's high time we had some real happiness around here!"

With that, they raised their glasses, and even John joined in, kissing Laney on the cheek and thumping Sam with gusto. He offered Sam the carriage for a Christmas Eve ride alone with Laney while he and his parents played a board game with the Williamses. "Consider it a Christmas present," he told Sam privately as they walked out together to check the team. "It's the best I have to give ya."

Sam never felt so fully blessed as he did that night in the carriage with Laney. Warm in their coats and robes, skimming along the snow on a starlit Christmas Eve, harness bells twinkling and horses prancing, they seemed to be in a fairyland or a painting. And yet, when he stopped the rig in a snowy grove and kissed her, when he held her close and brushed her cheeks and mouth with his lips and ran his fingers through her hair, she was as warm and real as anything he had ever touched. He slipped a pearl ring on her finger that Sister Chadester had lent him, an heirloom that had belonged to her mother. "I think it came across the plains," he said, "so it's old and precious, a symbol of another time. Someday you'll have your own, but I hope, for now, this ring will connect us to each other and to those who came before."

Laney twisted the white pearl on her finger. "It's beautiful," she said and eyed him curiously. "It doesn't seem that old to me at all. You're extraordinarily caught up in a pensive mood tonight. It's as if you're some-where else, another place, another time . . ."

"Maybe I'll make my presence better felt," he exclaimed, eagerly smothering her again with kisses, until she pushed him away, laughing happily.

"I've learned so much since coming here," he whispered, settling back against the seat. "I've learned what it means to be a man, to find your place, to take pride in your work, to serve other people, to serve God. A man's gotta fix his life so he can do that with whatever talents the Lord's given him. Most of all, I've discovered what it means to love a woman." Sam turned to face her, trembling as he spoke. "And, do you know, Laney, it's all tied up together. All of it. That's what I've learned. We work and serve and love and grow from one generation to the next for moments such as this. We live to see someone like Joey give his belt to Annabelle, or John donate the Saxon, or the town turn out to save the Sullivan hay or Heber Golby's barn. We exist for those moments. They teach us something about joy."

Laney lowered her eyes. "You've seen evil here too, Sam. Mick Sullivan's murdering both his brother and his friend."

"I know. Maybe being close to that has made me more aware of what's important—how human sorrow really hurts, how wickedness offends, how much better it is to be a John Chadester in this world—not letting shallowness and jealousy control your life even when you've lost your favorite car and your favorite girl."

"You've learned all that by coming to our town?" said Laney impishly. She'd heard enough serious musings for one night.

"Okay, okay." Sam laughed, taking her in his arms again. "Now, where were we?"

"We were right here." She rubbed her nose against his. "And besides, who said I was John's favorite girl? He never told me that!"

"Well, it's too late now." Sam kissed her with enthusiastic zest before she could say another word.

Chapter Eleven

A RAGING BLIZZARD BLEW OUT of the canyon two weeks after Christmas and smothered Alpine and the surrounding area with enough snow to cover roads, fence posts, and telephone wires. Rural mailboxes and familiar landmarks were obliterated in a sea of white. Milk froze before it could be delivered, and disoriented livestock died, unable to reach feeding troughs. The snow flew sideways under the force of the wind, which whistled off the benches, bitterly stinging everything it touched, including cheeks and noses and even fingers left bare for tying shoes or fastening buckles. Most people stayed shut in their houses, hoping that the weather would break before the wood ran out. School closed, and local businesses were shuttered. Even church services were canceled on the middle Sunday of the storm. Jack Harper, who lived closest to the chapel, climbed the steeple stairs to raise a red flag signaling the decision: "Say your prayers at home until the wind dies down."

Bishop Moroni Chadester prayed often as the blizzard raged. He nervously paced like a caged lion across his parlor floor. For long hours he sat by his window, looking out at the relentless storm and driving a clenched fist into his palm.

At the dinner table, he was no less impatient. "What if they need me?" he said more than once to Meg, as she passed him the meat and potatoes. "What if someone needs me?"

"Who needs you, Rone? Everyone's shut up at home just like we are, till the storm passes."

Sam and John both looked up from their plates, wondering if the bishop had heard anything from the Williamses' house. Sam hadn't seen Laney in days, and the telephone lines were down.

"Well, there's Eleanor Sullivan," said Bishop Rone. "What about Eleanor? That baby might come anytime. And Jim Peavey's been sick since Christmas. You know very well that Sister Runyan's been ailin'. Heber Golby's cows are always gettin' out of that makeshift stable he's got them in."

"Tilda Cottom's half a mile from the Sullivans if the baby comes," said Meg. "The rest of 'em will get by. Honestly, Rone, ya can't burden yourself with the whole world every time a blizzard blows through."

"It ain't the whole world that worries me," said Chadester with a wink, "just the ward."

"Yes," said Meg, casting a knowing glance at John. "That's worry enough."

"How long do you figure to keep the mercantile closed?" asked Sam, thinking of Laney. "Folks might be needing goods."

"I'm sure they do, but if they can't get to town, there's no use tempting them to try. I don't want to see anyone get caught out in this storm, including my employees. Most everyone I know has enough food in reserve. Anything they can get at the mercantile is something that can wait. It's other things I worry about, like medicine and doctorin' and such . . . and most of all, the things a bishop's good for. That's my stewardship, even in a storm . . . especially in a storm."

Three more days went by, and Sam was ready to join Bishop Rone in his pacing, so anxious was he to see Laney. He wasn't worried about her, as Chadester was about his congregation, but the days were impossibly long without her smile, her voice, her touch. "I *must* be in love," he told John frankly. "I can't stand time without her anymore."

"You're a goner," answered John. "There's no two ways about it."

They spent cold hours in the barn, puttering with the machinery, sharpening blades, and fixing broken tools. Sam began to disassemble Bishop Chadester's Ford, which needed some work before it would run again.

"Pa was one of the first in Alpine to own an automobile," said John. "He likes it but finds horses more dependable out here in the country. Maybe that'll change as more roads get paved."

"And maybe you'll get another Saxon someday too."

John only shrugged and smiled. Some dreams come around just once.

The following night the boys were awakened by a thudding at their bedroom door. John's father was there with a lantern and told them to get up and dressed. He needed them to go with him to the Williamses' place, and it couldn't wait until morning. A chill ran through Sam that was colder than the ice that crusted the windows, but Chadester immediately set his mind at ease.

"It's not Laney. At least, I don't think it is. I just have a feeling I've got to go there, a strong prompting, so to speak. More than likely, it's the boy. He's sick again and needs a blessing." He put his hand on Sam's shoulder. "I need you fellas to help me get through the snow."

Even with all of these assurances, Sam's heart was pounding as he dressed and pulled on his boots. Sister Chadester, in her housecoat, filled them with hot Brigham tea in the kitchen and kept a wary eye on the weather outside as John struck another lantern.

"It's two miles to Kit's as the crow flies," said the bishop. "We can't make out the road or the fence posts anyhow, so we might as well strike out across the fields."

"But you'll run into the sloughs by the south boundary," warned Meg. "You'll sink down sure as anything in the dark. You ought to go at first light, Rone. It's too risky now."

"We'll be careful and find our way around the sloughs. I can't wait."

On the porch they tied snowshoes to their feet and took ski poles down from hooks against the wall. Sam and John held the lanterns on opposite sides as the trio made its way into the wintry blast in front of them. Meg, wrapped in a shawl, stood watching on the porch until the three of them turned to distant shadows beneath the cold stars.

Sam didn't mind the cold. He was glad to be going, tramping across that drift-bound field toward a good cause and what he cared for most. The wind bit at his cheeks and nose. Snow frosted his eyelashes. The snowshoes were wooden and awkward and didn't tie on very well. He wasn't used to them. But he threw his chest out and swung his lantern, as if to say, "Go ahead and blow at me, you darned old wind. My girl's out there in the night, and no storm's gonna keep me from her."

He watched Bishop Chadester and admired the man beyond words. Bishop Rone had no girl to save, no damsel in distress. He had received some prompting from the Lord, a summons he didn't completely understand, and here he was, showing simple faith in a whisper from the still, small voice, even one that came in the middle of a stormy night about a neighbor two miles away. No, Sam didn't mind being part of this crew. If the cold wind of experience made a boy a man, he was growing by the minute.

The wide, latticed snowshoes kept the men from sinking through the crust of the snow as they crossed the frozen acres where drifts newly scalloped by the wind changed every fixed direction. A grove of bare elms, creaking noisily on the left, helped them gauge their position, and they moved toward the sound, familiar with the corner where the trees were clustered. From there they headed south—or rather what they thought was south—squinting for a gatepost or a pinch of light.

Then the moment they dreaded came. It happened just as success seemed almost within their reach. Bishop Chadester had spotted a glimmer a quarter of a mile through the darkness, like a single star just topping the farthest hill. "That's the Williams place!" he shouted into the wind and eagerly plowed ahead.

Sam heard a loud crack and in the beam of his light saw Chadester tumble forward several yards in front of him.

"Pa!" John cried, lunging ahead, his lantern swinging violently with every heavy stride. Bishop Rone had sunk into a hidden slough, striking a thick, dead cedar branch on the way down, splitting his snowshoe in half and badly injuring his ankle. He was writhing in pain and frustration when the boys reached him at the bottom of the gully.

"We got ya, Pa. We got ya," John lifted his father up against the bank of snow and looked into his eyes, as Sam tried to steady the lantern.

"Cursed be the devil!" Rone Chadester spat. "Your ma warned me to watch out for them sloughs. Don't you go tellin' her I slipped into one."

John tore off what remained of the broken snowshoe and carefully removed his father's boot, keeping the foot and stocking dry. "She's already swollen up like a boiled plum. I think it's broken, Pa." He slathered the ankle with snow. The leg was gray and purple in the lantern gleam, and John didn't want his father looking at it. He wrapped his muffler around the foot and ankle, making certain every bare inch was covered. Then he took one of the ski poles and tied it against Chadester's ankle as a brace. Forced to remove his gloves to work, his fingers soon turned red and stiff, and he frequently blew on his hands to keep them nimble. Sam looked on, holding the light and measuring the pain in the bishop's twisted face.

"Can you get me to the Williamses' place?" Chadester groaned. "Can you still see their lights?"

"We'll get ya there, Pa. Don't you fret." John put a ski pole in each of his father's hands. Then he and Sam, on either side, lifted him beneath his shoulders. He was a heavy man, especially in fur and woolens, and he carried a weight of snow as he rose, but the boys were young and strong, and together they managed to support him while he gained his balance.

Unable to climb the bank, they were forced to remain in the slough until it leveled out enough to let them move unimpeded across the pasture. By then, the lights at the Williamses' house were brighter, the actual distance more defined. Bishop Chadester was struggling, but the proximity offered hope.

"Sorry I got you out here, boys," he moaned at one point. "You didn't need this."

"Nonsense, Pa," said John. "What was ya gonna do in that slough all by yourself?"

When they finally dragged themselves onto Kit Williams's porch, it was Johanna who opened the door. "Oh, thank God!" she cried. "Thank God! Thank God!" Tears were running down her cheeks. She drew the wanderers in and slipped to her knees as Laney and her father hurried into the room in shock—both at the bishop's condition and the fact that he was there at all.

"We've been praying that you'd come!" Johanna's cries continued, as the boys helped Chadester to the daybed in the parlor, where Joey often slept. "We pleaded with the Lord, and here you are!"

"I'm afraid I'm not much good to you in the shape I'm in," the bishop apologized. "I'm the one in need this time."

Laney had rushed to Sam the moment she saw him, and now the emergencies for both families became clear.

"It's Joey," she explained. "For three days now he's been getting weaker. He can't eat. He can't drink. He can hardly breathe. We've been locked in here by the storm with no doctor and no help for him. Oh, Sam, what are we to do?" She buried her face against him and trembled in his arms.

"We're here now, Laney." Sam held the back of her head in his palm and comforted her. "Lean on me. We'll both lean on the Lord."

"Just havin' your presence in the house is bound to bring us solace," said Kit Williams gratefully to Chadester. "You're the Lord's own steward in this valley. That you'd find your way to us through the snow and storm shows the power of your faith and ours. We'll never forget you, Bishop Rone, whatever happens. But it pains me that ya had to get crippled up to come to us."

Chadester leaned forward wearily on one of the ski poles, which was still in his hand, as he sat hunched over on the daybed. "It's humbling that me or mine would be the answer to anybody's prayer. A broken ankle is a small price to pay for such a callin'. We'll try to help your boy."

While John and Johanna tended to Bishop Rone, bringing a tub of medicinal salts to bathe his leg and keep the swelling down, the others surrounded a listless Joey in the bedroom. Sam was shocked by what he saw. Joey was a ghost, as frail and gray as death itself, lying in a fetal position with only an occasional rasp of breath to signal any life in him at all. The kerosene lamp near his pillow cast an amber glow across his face that reminded Sam of an old tintype he had once seen in an antique shop. The boy in the picture seemed to be looking straight out of the past.

Joey's eyes were closed, except when Laney's pleading aroused him. "Joey, Joey, Sam's here. Can you say hello to Sam?" Then the eyelids would widen slightly, and the boy would raise his hand so that Sam could hold it. For a long time, he tousled the boy's hair, pressed a cloth to his clammy forehead, and listened to his labored breath, which grew weaker as the minutes passed. For all the ministering of the others, only Laney was able to rouse him, but even her efforts grew less effective. He was a round ball, rolled up in the womb of his bed, topped by his pretty curls.

*   *   *

An hour went by, and as the family continued to minister to Joey, a new crisis arose. Sam sat at Bishop Chadester's side in a state of fright. "They want *me* to bless the boy!" he whispered hoarsely. "They want *me* to give him a priesthood blessing. I can't do it, Bishop Rone. I can't give them what they want."

"You've got the Melchizedek priesthood, don't you?" said Chadester.

"Yes, but—"

"John doesn't yet. He hasn't been on a mission like you have."

"But I'm not you. They prayed for *you* to come, not me."

"They prayed for help and priesthood power. You can give them both."

Bishop Chadester leaned back against the top of the bed and looked squarely at Sam. "You know, I was reminded of something earlier as I lay here thinking about things. I'm a bishop and my duties are important, but two strong, young fellows stood on either side of me tonight and got me through the storm. They may not have my experience yet, nor the wisdom that comes with it, but I'd have shriveled up and died without their help, and that's for sure." Chadester paused, and there was a light in his eye. "You've got the same power I do, Sam, and Kit Williams needs you to take your place as part of this family. You'll marry Laney soon. It's time to show you're worthy of her. Now, unless you've done some things you shouldn't have lately, unless you're somehow unworthy, you get in there and use the priesthood to give that boy a blessing."

Sam was trembling. "But he's dying, Bishop. Joey's dying."

"Just let the Spirit lead you, Sam. The words will come to you." Chadester bowed his head, put his hand over Sam's, and the two men prayed. Then Sam stood and faced what he'd been asked to do with a confidence he'd never had before.

In the shadowy room, with the family circling the bed, Laney and her mother weeping, and John steadying them with his strong arms, Kit Williams laid his hands on his ravaged little son, consecrating him with oil, before turning the "voice" portion of the blessing over to his son-in-law-to-be. Years later, Sam would remember the moment and wonder how he found the strength.

"Joseph Kenneth Williams, in the name of Jesus Christ and by the power of the holy Melchizedek priesthood, which I bear, I lay my hands upon your head and bless you. I feel moved, dear Joey, to release you from your pain, to free you from the chains of disability that have shackled you. In spite of the deep anguish it will bring to those who love you, I feel moved to free you; I feel moved to let you go." Sam heard Laney stifle an audible gasp, and he hesitated. Her agony cut through him. He ached for a different miracle, but he had only this one to give. "Tomorrow, you'll stand straight and tall," he told Joey, his voice rising. "You'll run like other boys. You'll talk and read and form fine sentences, and all the love you have for your sister and your parents will come spilling forth. You'll look down from where you are and wonder why we mortals kept you here so long, when you were an angel meant to fly. We love you, Joey. We send you to the Father. He will protect you until we meet again . . ." The circle stood in silence, clasping each other's hands, while the lamp by young Joey's bedside burned low and finally lost its flame.

* * *

Joseph Kenneth Williams did indeed pass through the veil within hours of the blessing in the amber-lit, snow-covered house in Alpine. Sam pondered the experience and his part in it for many days as the storm abated and life returned to normal. Joey's death was inevitable that night; Sam's prayer had probably done very little in hastening it along, and no miraculous healing was within his power. But he also remembered the warmth that filled him when he pronounced the blessing, how his fingers trembled, and how the words were not his own. Perhaps his priesthood, that symbol of his maturity, was a conduit for divine love along with its more authoritative functions. By this time he had forgotten about the smartphone and its need to be connected to something greater than itself, but the message became clear without the metaphor.

Eleanor Sullivan gave birth to a baby boy the same day they buried Joey Williams. This vivid reminder of the constant cycle of life was not lost on either family, and Johanna made certain that leftover food from the funeral lunch was taken to feed the Sullivan children. Eleanor named her baby Joseph, although most people had expected him to be named for his father. "This baby will always remind us of another little boy," explained the widow.

After the funeral services, which were delayed by ground too frozen to dig a grave, John and Sam spent a week in Provo, where Bishop Chadester required surgery on his ankle, and Meg decided it was a good time to catch up on annual supplies for both the mercantile and the ward. She used the boys for hauling and driving the team, and by the time Sam returned to Alpine, the weather had cleared enough to plant a wooden cross at Joey's mound. Kit Williams prayed at the spot as the families stood beside him.

Laney and Sam returned there alone two weeks later when they could ponder the resting place by themselves. "Do you know I almost hated you when you consigned Joey to death that night?" said Laney, her eyes filled with guilt. The air was clear and sharp. The mountains cut a snowy edge against the sky. The sun had shone enough that tufts of grass peeked through the frost around the grave. "I expected you to use your priesthood powers to make him well. I wasn't looking for a miracle. I didn't expect you to say, 'Take up thy bed and walk,' but I didn't want him to die."

"I know, Laney." Kneeling, Sam put his arm around her and held her close. "I know what you wanted me to do." They stayed there, bent in silence, looking at the cross. Kit Williams promised a granite marker soon, with Joey's name engraved on it, but the wooden cross would do for a while.

Finally, Laney looked up into Sam's eyes. "But I don't hate you, Sam. I never did. I never could. What you said in the prayer was right and for the best, and I will love you for it all my days." She took from her coat the blue-and-purple beaded belt that Joey had painstakingly created and given to Annabelle, who had befriended him so eagerly. "Annabelle gave this back to me the other day and told me to put it on Joey's grave."

Sam helped her to her feet, and Laney hung the concho belt in all its glory. "He did a great job with those beads." She looked at the belt and smiled. "Crooked is creative," she repeated. "The beads were what he had."

River Rising

May 22, 1916—Oh, the storms that still come back to befall us, even after the scourge of winter passes. Past sins still unaccounted for still plague us yet in tragic ways. We've had a cruel spring run-off, let's start with that—water gushing from the canyons, enough to cover Pharaoh's host. And to think that such a blessing would spit out our iniquities and our joys together, and leave us trembling in its wake.

Moroni Chadester Journal

Chapter Twelve

As THE WEDDING DAY APPROACHED, Sam viewed his world and himself from a new perspective. He could have sworn he'd grown several inches since the fall, though a tape measure would prove otherwise. His shoulders felt broad, his firm jaw set and confident. The fields and pastures he looked upon, the horizons he surveyed, the future he anticipated—all of them stood out in striking relief whenever he paused to consider his good fortune. It was spring, with the potential for new life and abundance everywhere, and enough buoyancy in his heart to conquer every doubt or obstacle. "Oh, to be young again"—Bishop Rone slapped him on the shoulder one day—"and so full of fearlessness and self-reliance!"

The wedding was to be in the Salt Lake Temple, with a dance that evening at the ward house in Alpine. The fuss over lace and ruffles and invitations and music didn't bother Sam. In fact, he relished being part of such a grand celebration, and for Laney's sake, he went along with every minor detail that she and Johanna envisioned necessary for the success of the occasion. When John ribbed him about the tuxedo he would have to wear and the hours he would have to stand, greeting "smothering grandmothers and slobbering babies," Sam wouldn't give an inch.

"I'd stand stock still in a straight-jacket for Laney," Sam declared, "and so would you."

"You're right. I would," John conceded, and Sam immediately regretted his last remark. But John took a jab at him and was soon laughing again, and goodwill resumed.

Sam worked with the Chadesters that spring to earn his rent on a brick cottage Bishop Rone owned in town, where Sam and Laney would live after the wedding. He helped wean new calves and repair old fences, in addition to the planting.

"You're strong, and you can buck a bale," said Chadester. "You proved that last fall. But you ain't what I call husky. I see more of a city boy in you sometimes, a well-dressed, merchant type. Maybe I'll try you out at managing the store and let you help us out on the side when we get busy in the fields. How does that sound?"

"That sounds just fine," said Sam, pleased that he had earned the bishop's confidence. "Thank you, sir."

So with these plans falling into place, a final lark into the mountains became a focus for Sam. He wanted to spend some time alone with Laney before the wedding day, and a summer canyon seemed the perfect destination, an escape to nature to forever mark the end of their courting days. He had long believed there was nothing more arrestingly attractive than a beautiful girl riding a beautiful horse. It had not escaped his memory that the first time he'd laid eyes on Laney, she was astride her dappled pony. They would ride the trail up into the canyon, up to Tibble Creek and Granite Flats, as far as they could go. They would watch the American Fork River race down its twisting path, sweeping like a froth of silver at its highest point.

The mountain snows had been heavy and wet and slow to melt. Warm weather had come suddenly, and now the canyon spilled its treasure with more speed and volume than the irrigation ditches could absorb. Emergency canals were opened to accommodate the extra water and prevent flooding in the valley, but above them, near the mouth of the canyon, the scene was one of splendor as the water found its outlet and surged into foothills below.

"The aspens and the maple trees are all green now," he told Laney. "The segos are blossoming."

Laney usually wore a long, wide skirt, even for riding, but just lately she'd been taken with the new fashion of lady's trousers, which were snug and belted at the waist but flared slightly at the knee, where they were tucked into fitted boots and leggings. Sam liked the look. It was handy for riding, and it showed off Laney's trim figure, which always pleased him. She wore a loose, cream-colored blouse and long blue sailor's tie on top— the image of the attractive tomboy, with her single braid. They packed a lunch of sandwiches and dried fruit in their saddle bags, took a canteen of lemonade, and struck out early while the sun was still climbing between the peaks above them.

Moving first along the country lanes they knew, Laney challenged him to race to a point where the farthest range fence ended, and he took the dare. It was a foolish choice. Laney was light in the saddle and had been riding since she was a child. She was fearless on a horse and soon had Blossom galloping at full stride. She beat Sam by half a length, passing the fence post with a victory cry. They finally prodded their horses upward onto the benches, looking back over a valley that spoke of Eden, although it was more a desert than a meadow in the literal sense. "Any place you are is Eden, if you're loved," said Laney, when Sam mentioned the difference.

"And if you bring enough water to it," he replied with an ironic wink.

"Well, we certainly have enough water this year." Laney brushed off his sarcasm, looking down from her vantage point at the river flowing from the canyon, filling the ditches and canals, and turning every piece of foliage lush and green. "But never enough love," she added, stretching across her saddle to kiss him. "There's never enough of that."

Sam leaned eagerly toward her to reach her lips and nearly fell from his horse as her pony stepped farther away.

Laughing, Laney apologized, "I'm sorry. I think my father trained this horse to protect me from mashers on the road."

"We'll have to buy a car—as soon as possible."

She moved ahead of him. The cleft of the canyon widened, and they moved into the shade of its walls. Shrub oak and juniper hung from every crag and crevice above them; trees hugged the riverbanks and cast a bowery of leaves across the narrow places. Soon they passed the trail to the Timpanogos caves, where men with lanterns could venture into the darkness and come back with tales of Indian brides and the "Heart of the Mountain." Laney had never been inside the caves, but Bishop Chadester had. He believed that someday the trail would be improved and electricity brought to the caves so people could go on guided tours and see the wonders of the earth. Laney thought she'd wait until that day came before she took the chance of getting lost inside.

Everywhere on the passing trail, they could hear the rush of water. Even where the riverbed was usually narrow, the power of the rapids had sliced away the banks and furrowed deeper into the rock-strewn bottom until there were places where the trail twisted under a flow of branches and debris. Sometimes the water reached the knees or bellies of the horses, and much of the ride became a constant search for the dry part of the path. But in the end the view proved worth the effort. From the highest places where they could pause, slide down from their saddles, and let the horses stray into the forest, the landscape spread before them like a dream. The sounds of nature serenaded them, and they were one with it. The crisp air invigorated them. Slabs of snow still frosted the glens and shady ridges, and the world below shimmered under its ice-blue dome of heaven.

They found a spot to eat their lunch, on some smooth boulders beneath a limber pine, and propped the picnic there. Sam watched the wisps of stray hair blow off Laney's cheeks as she prepared the sandwiches.

"You'll never change from what you are right now," he said suddenly.

She looked up, smiling. "What do you mean? Of course I'll change. Everybody does."

He was wistful, starry-eyed, in love. "No, for me, you'll always be as you are right now, whatever the future brings."

Laney stopped what she was doing and moved toward him, snuggling under his arm and laying her head against his chest. "You're being awfully mysterious today. What makes you talk like that?"

"Like what? I love you. That's all I know."

"Sometimes you seem so . . . so . . . well, so otherworldly. Like you're from a distant place. I know that's ridiculous, and I don't mean it literally, but I get the feeling you're here . . . well . . . temporarily, sometimes."

"Temporarily?"

"I love you so much, I think sometimes you can't be real," Laney admitted, "that you'll leave me too soon, as Joey did. Our love is so deep, I fear it's temporary, made for this time, but not *all* time. Do you know what I mean? I lost him, and someday, I'll lose you."

A jolt of panic shot through Sam's heart. He sat up straight, his hands on her shoulders. "No, no, no! Don't ever say that! I don't know what came over me just then, with all that vague nonsense about some abstract future. I love you, and I will forever. The temple will seal us for eternity, and I intend to keep those covenants." Sam spread his arm wide, taking in the vista before them. "This is our world, Laney. This is our time and place. Let's not ever talk of distance and loss again."

Laney nodded and kissed him gently. "All right," she said. "I promise."

After lunch they packed the saddlebags and staked the horses in the alpine meadow, hoping to hike farther up the ridge line. Soon they were tracing along hidden pathways, framed by rising walls of pine and quaking aspen. They passed a fellow hiker, a lone man with a walking stick headed in the opposite direction and singing.

He ceased his tune and nodded to them. "A beautiful day for it," he said, throwing out his chest, and Sam pleasantly tipped his hat. "I thought I had the trail to myself till I saw you two. You've got a treat ahead of you. There's a swinging bridge up yonder that's quite a thrill." They passed by him, and he took up his song again. His voice soon faded as he vanished down the trail.

In no time at all they found the bridge. It stretched only about thirty feet, not far, and was strung together with thick rope on either side and anchored by wooden poles. The bridge's base was made up of flat boards woven together with another set of ties. It sagged slightly in the middle, and not far below the sag, the river gushed and frothed like wild Neptune raging at the boulders in his path. "Look at that," said Sam. "The middle of that bridge will offer quite a view—if you dare go out there."

"Why wouldn't I?" said Laney, testing one end of the rope. "It seems secure enough, and our singing mountain man recommended it."

Sam grinned at her. "You always were rather fearless for a girl."

She punched him playfully with her fist. "What will you give me if I make it all the way across and back again with absolutely no help from you?"

"And no tears or pleading for rescue when you're stranded in the middle?"

"No tears or pleading."

"I'll give you the moon and stars," said Sam, only half in jest; with all his heart he wished he could fulfill the bargain. He kissed her lightly for good luck and watched her as she tentatively grasped the hand line on both sides and stepped onto the bridge.

The boards at Laney's feet were wobbly and uneven, but she soon found the proper gait. "You can see the water between the slats," she called back over her shoulder. "The open space is wider than you think." The ropes swayed beneath her weight, and Sam swallowed hard a time or two when she wasn't looking at him. She kept her eyes down most of the time, balancing and clutching the side ropes tightly.

In the middle, where the bridge sagged to its lowest point, Laney stopped to take in the view. "It's lovely here," she called. "You can follow the river for miles, although it hides itself sometimes." When Sam made a gesture as if to join her, she put up her hand to stop him. "No, you can come in a minute. I'm finishing on my own."

He stepped back and watched her come to the end of the intrepid journey, stepping up on the other side and turning to face him with her arms outstretched. "There! I did it! Who said women are no fun?"

He nodded his approval of her courage, anxious to cross the bridge himself, but willing to wait for her to finish the other half of the bargain. "Take your time," he teased her, as she lingered on the other side. "Catch your breath. Gather your courage. The first time might have been beginner's luck, you know."

Laney looked about, playfully ignoring him. The incline on her side was steep, with crevices and boulders squeezing the narrow trail as it twisted downhill away from the bridge and disappeared in the underbrush.

"I'm sure this path follows the river," she finally called. "Once you're over here, I don't think we'll have to cross again, at least not until we trek all the way down and find our horses."

"Come on back," said Sam, listening to the music of the racing water crashing under him. "You're not getting out of a second run. Once over, once back. That was the deal."

"Okay, okay, I'm coming." Laney moved toward the bridge. "Let's hope it can hold us both at once."

She was three feet from the bridge, about to reach for the anchor rope, when suddenly a figure appeared in front of her. He wore a crumpled slouch hat and a heavy coat and came out of a crevice between the rocks so abruptly that Laney jumped back in fright.

Across the river Sam blinked in surprise, thinking he had seen a ghost. The man was short and stubby, unshaven, with narrow, watery eyes. Sam's mouth dropped open. It was Mick Sullivan, looking like he'd just come out of hibernation, with a small ax and a rucksack. He looked at Laney, confused, and then across at Sam, and a dull recognition slowly flooded his sullen face.

Chapter Thirteen

"Why, I know you," he barked at Laney, suddenly five inches away. "You're Kit Williams's girl, the one with the funny-shaped brother. He was teched and had feet for legs, as I recall. He scaddled around on a wagon like a little puppy dog, which is about all the sense he had."

In a frenzy of reflexive anger, Laney swung her fist ineffectively at Mick's jaw and shrieked when he grabbed her by the collar. Across the river, Sam cursed and yelled and leaped toward the bridge.

Pulling a struggling Laney with him, Sullivan moved toward the anchor ropes and began chopping at them with his ax. Desperately, Laney pummeled his arm, beat his shoulders, and tried to fight him for the ax. He finally knocked her to the ground with a backhand swipe and returned to his work unimpeded. Sam was at the middle of the bridge when the bottom rope snapped from its pole, and all he could do was fight to keep his balance as the bridge tipped dangerously.

With no one to resist him, Sullivan made short work of the other anchor rope, and soon the entire contraption swung like a flying trapeze against the opposite bank. Sam clung to it, gasping, bracing himself as he hit the side. Barely surviving the jolt, he scratched and clawed for anything to grab, finally wedging his arms and elbows between the footboards and gripping the ropes that bound the slats together. Below his feet the water surged, churning and whipping the end of the bridge that dangled in the waves. He heard Laney shrieking his name, and he twisted his head to see both Sullivan and Laney gaping at his plight—she with terror in her eyes, he with a sullen curl across his lips.

The rope was knotted between the footboards, and slowly, carefully, Sam worked to grasp each knot above him until he reached the anchor poles. Struggling at the top, his legs slipped twice before he finally found the strength to lift himself off the dangling bridge onto the path again. There he scrambled to his feet and turned to face Sullivan and Laney across the sharp divide. He was still breathing hard, still shaking, but he saw relief on Laney's face, and it strengthened him.

Sullivan only smiled in a scornful way and stood back, considering the situation. "Well, ain't this a fine howdayado!" he shouted. "Never in my life have I ever ended up on the good side of anything—until today!" They stared at each other, the three of them, speechless for a moment, while Mick looked from Laney to Sam and back again and moved around with his chin in the air like a banty rooster. "No," he chortled, "I never expected anything so rich as this."

Sam's eyes flew from Sullivan to Laney. He fought for self-control. Laney was standing as far away as she could get from Sullivan, up against some rocks that skirted the narrow approach to the bridge. There was nowhere to go. She seemed almost resigned to some unknown terror and never took her eyes off Sam.

It was more than Sam could take. "Sullivan, please." He stretched out his hand, begging. "You've brought a lot of pain to people when you probably didn't mean to. Don't make it worse. Laney's done nothing to you. Go on your way and let her be. You've hidden out for a long time now, and no one's ever found you. You hurt this girl, everyone will be on your trail again, and this time, they aren't gonna quit."

Sullivan laughed and walked toward Laney, having apparently made up his mind. He ripped the sailor's tie from around her collar and used it to bind her wrists. She resisted but only slightly now. Her cheeks still burned. Fear subdued her. She stared across at Sam, her eyes wide, almost trance-like. He could hardly bear that look, clenching his fists and pacing and trying to tell her without speaking that everything would be all right. He would save her. Like some gallant knight of old, he would find a way to swoop down and rescue the fair princess. Yet the water rushed and the chasm gaped between them and a killer laughed and cackled at their plight.

"I guess the whole town wonders why I murdered George," said Sullivan, as he knotted the tie on Laney's wrists. "He was a good man, they thought, a good brother to a drunk like me." Mick pulled Laney toward him and spoke directly to her. "The truth is, I didn't have no notion of killin' George in the barn that night. I went to ask him for some money. He told me no, said he'd given me enough all ready. There he was, all high and mighty, with a barn and plenty of hay to graze his animals, a nice house for his family, and that wife of his who never liked me even speakin' to her children. George had all he needed. He looked at me like I was scum, just 'cause I didn't have his slick and gentlemanly ways with folks. 'Ya got to get a hold of yourself, Mick,' is what he said. 'Ya got to quit the bottle. I ain't givin' ya no more money till ya do.' George musta told me that a hundred times. That night in the barn I just got hot about it, sick of always being the black-sheep brother everybody hated or felt sorry for. I let George have it with that knife, and I tossed it in the field. I didn't mean to do it. Something just come over me, that's all."

While Sullivan rambled, Sam was frantically looking for a way to cross the gap. Keeping the man focused on all his alleged injustices seemed a good way to play for time. Maybe another traveler would pass, an officer or someone with a gun. He thought of inching down the steep bank and jumping into the surging water. The river wasn't wide at this point, only swift and cold, but probably deeper than it looked. If he was swept downstream or trapped by the current . . . it was too great a risk. He was desperate to keep Laney where he could see her. If Sullivan took her into the backcountry, finding them quickly would be impossible.

"What about Lester Hawkins?" he yelled at Sullivan. "I thought he was your friend."

"Yeah, he was," said Sullivan sadly. "I hate what I done to him. But he was gonna turn that knife in, don't ya see? Bishop Rone had told about the fingerprints and all, and I knew I was a goner if they got that knife. I saw my chance and took off runnin', but Lester tried to stop me. He couldn't figure out what I was tellin' him. He thought I was just scared, that's all. I had to poke him with the knife for him to let me be. It was a while before I found out that he died. I didn't think I'd cut him deep."

Sam stared across at Laney. There was no way for him to cross the river at that point, and they all knew it.

Sullivan slung his rucksack on his back and picked up his ax. "I ain't gonna let no law take me. I'll use the girl here for a few days till I'm good and clear of 'em again. You tell 'em to stay away, and she'll be all right. From the very first, I never meant to hurt nobody." He had pulled Laney toward him again, and now he brushed her cheek. "Just every once in a while something comes over me, and I can't help myself. You know how it is." With that, he walked away toward the narrow trail that led into the brush, jerking Laney behind him. She looked back at Sam and whispered his name before the trees and brush covered up the path. They vanished into the thickening of rocks and forest before Sam could do anything.

Sam leaped to keep pace in the same direction on his side. He struggled to listen for sounds of them thrashing through the underbrush after they were out of sight. He tried to glimpse them at any opening in the trees. The rush of the water below was all he heard, but he saw flashes of movement in the leaves on the far slope, and soon he determined that their trail, like his, followed the river.

He stumbled forward, racing downhill, oblivious to gullies and rocks and branches and the danger of sudden twists and bends on the uneven path. He came to where the water had puddled the road and recklessly splashed through it so fast he risked falling headlong down the slope. But panic beckoned him, and he couldn't help himself.

At a cross point where a trail marker stood, he saw the older man they had passed earlier, the one who had greeted them with a song. Sam shouted, and the fellow looked up with a puzzled expression and then recovered enough to catch Sam as he slid to a stop.

"Find an officer!" Sam cried. "Find a warden, a ranger, some kind of law officer. A killer has kidnapped my girl!"

Startled, the man tried to calm Sam down, to be certain of his information, but he had seen Laney earlier, and it didn't take him long to realize this was no joke. "There's a ranger station a mile below. I think they have a telephone. We'll get some help, young man. Don't you worry, now. We'll get some help." He anxiously set off, but when Sam didn't follow, he turned back, catching up to grab Sam's arm. With nervous hesitation, he ran his tanned fingers through his white hair. "Listen, son, from what you say, this is serious business. You can't handle this alone. Come on with me and get some help."

"If you'll bring help back, I'd be much obliged," said Sam hoarsely. "I can't leave her on this mountain. I've got to stay as close as I can. I've got to keep some track of where they are."

"I understand." After a brief nod, the man abruptly turned and started down the path.

The trail marker pointed the way to another bridge, and Sam soon found it and crossed the river, feeling considerable progress in being on the same side of the stream as Sullivan and Laney. Now he listened for sounds, searched the pathways, looked for vantage points. He decided to climb into the rocks and boulders clustered above the tree line in the canyon.

From there he could spot movement on the trails below and hopefully determine Sullivan's position.

He chose a likely ridge which featured a granite slope above it and probably enough stones and ledges for the purpose. With adrenaline to spare, he muscled up to the ridge, breathing hard when he reached it but looking back on the river and the trees as if he had conquered gravity.

Suddenly, he saw them. Laney and Sullivan were there by the side of the river, walking along a patch of gravel, the one place where there weren't any trees. Laney's wrists were still bound, and Sullivan was pushing her from behind, apparently in some kind of game, trying to tease her into going near the water. The rapids there were not wide, but they were deep and full, lapping the edges of the sandy bar where Laney stood. Her head was bowed as Sullivan kept nudging her. But she looked as though she'd rather face the river than his greasy smile, so she kept her back to him and resisted his prodding by standing firm or moving stiffly as he pushed.

Sam immediately slid down the same path he had climbed, his heart pounding. He hurried through the brush and trees, listening for the rush of the river, taking a direct route to where he knew Laney would be. His anxiety made it seem much farther than he expected, and his strength was nearly gone when the sound of the waves and Sullivan's growing voice told him he'd made it. Slowing his pace and grabbing a thick limb lying on the ground, Sam burst through the trees and onto the gravel spread where Sullivan and Laney were.

"The law is coming for you, Mick! I'm here to take Laney home."

For a millisecond, both Sullivan and Laney were frozen where they stood, shocked at the sight of a trembling young man with a tree limb clutched in his hand. Laney's eyes flashed with utter gladness and relief, but Sullivan reacted first, grabbing her from behind and pressing a long blade against her throat.

"Back off, boy! I'll cut her! You know I'll do it too!"

Sam stopped in his tracks. He threw the tree limb to the ground. "Please," he begged. He found Laney's eyes and saw that they were locked on his. He knew she loved him. "You don't want to do this," he told Mick. "You don't want to be known for this."

Sullivan had eased a few steps back, dragging Laney with him. He was tired, it was plain. "Oh, heck. You're sayin' the truth. I *don't* want to do this. I don't want to be known for killin' a helpless woman while 'er hands are tied. That ain't right." He looked at the sky and muttered to himself.

"I'm sick of this. I'm sick of all of it. I'm sick of hiding out like a rat in these hills. You say the law's comin' for me? Well, let 'em come. I'm tired of runnin'. I really am." Sullivan lowered the knife still clutched in his fist. "I never meant to kill my brother. Something came over me, and it just happened!"

Sam took a step forward, watching Laney, who raised her bound hands to touch her throat. Sullivan was still holding her with one arm around the waist, but he seemed finished and ready to let go. Then he suddenly stiffened. He looked down at Laney and abruptly brushed his rough and whiskered jaw against her cheek.

Repulsed, she turned away, and the gesture sparked his last resolve. "I've always had a jealousy for other men and what they had," he yelled at Sam, and with that, he stepped back and let the ground fall out from underneath his boots, taking a screaming Laney with him into the surging stream.

Salt Lake County—Present Day

Awakening

Aggggggg! Aggggggg! *The patient groaned so loudly and so horribly that chills quivered up the spine of the attending nurse, although the shock of the man's sudden rise from his pillow was as frightening as the sound. Carroll, Samuel, in a deep coma seven weeks, according to his chart. Never so much as fluttered an eyelid, and now this. You don't see it often, but something jolted him. Listen to that. He's screaming. He's wild-eyed and screaming. The attendants are holding him down, poor guy. He's fighting them. He's calling a name. 'Laney' or 'Lanny,' it sounds like. Probably a family member. Won't they be surprised after all this time. I wonder where he thinks he's been, locked up in his mind like that. Well, it's time to bring him back to reality, whatever reality will be for him now that he's passed through a seven-week fog and come out the other end. I wonder if he'll remember his own name.*

Chapter Fourteen

"My gosh, Sam, I can't believe it!"

It was David. Five days had passed since Sam had awoken, and every hour was bringing him greater awareness and easing him away from pain. David threw his arms around his brother, propped against the pillow in his hospital bed.

"I can't believe it," he repeated. "I mean, of course I can! The Lord promises miracles sometimes, but, man, it's been so long . . ."

"That's what I hear," said Sam, fist bumping his brother. A thrill of joy went through him at the sound of David's voice. The room was white and clinical. A vertical window filled it with light. A silent television looked down at them from a gliding arm.

"I got here as soon as I could," said David, pulling up a chair. "I guess they told you, I've been in Mexico doing some work. Trish had trouble getting through when she tried to call with the news, and it was a while before I could get a flight home." He glanced around Sam's new room. "I know everyone has been here, Mom and Dad and everyone."

"They've made quite a fuss." Sam nodded. "Mom's been here every day. She spends most of the time crying. I guess everyone pretty much had my funeral planned. I've barely had a minute to figure out what happened."

"Do you remember anything?"

"About the accident, not much."

"Are you going to be okay?" David grinned and punched him. "Does everything work all right?"

Sam flexed his fingers and returned the smile. "Everything's a little stiff, since I haven't been moving around much lately, but the doctor says with exercise, I'll be as good as new in a few weeks. I'm starting rehabilitation tomorrow, and then we'll see."

David eyed him squarely. "What about your head, old man? Your brains get scrambled? Are we going to have to read everything for you from now on?"

"Naw, they've been runnin' lots of tests, but I can read. My eyes get tired in a hurry, though, and I'll probably need glasses. I'll earn the title. I'll be an old man before my time."

Sam saw sympathy in David's eyes. He knew he tired quickly. His chin was beginning to hang, and his shoulders were drooping. "Hey, that's okay," teased David. "Maybe you won't be such a smart aleck now." He hesitated, placing his hand on Sam's arm. "I'm going to let you rest. I'll be back later, and we can talk more about getting you on your feet." He gently patted Sam's cheek, and there was a tear in his eye as he spoke. "Love ya, brother. I've been sky high since Trish called. I'm awfully glad you came back to us."

"David," said Sam, as his brother was heading out the door, "you were reading me a journal while I was asleep, a journal by a bishop named Moroni Chadester from Alpine. Am I right?"

David turned back to the bed, dumbfounded. "Yes! Yes! Yes! Of course you're right! Do you remember that? I read you the whole thing. I didn't know if you could even hear me!"

"You still got that journal somewhere?"

"Well, sure, it's at home. Do you want to look at it again?"

"Yeah, I'd like that," said Sam. Sam wasn't sure how much of his experience there was actually part of the journal and how much was simply his own imagination, a fantasy prompted by what he was hearing David read. He wanted answers before he told anyone much of anything, and it was going to take a while.

*   *   *

"I'll be glad to read aloud to you again," said David when he brought the journal, "if you're eyes aren't up to it yet."

"Thanks," said Sam, "but I'd like to try this on my own."

Sam's eyes were weak, but reading Moroni Chadester's journal brought tears instead of weariness. He scoured every page and ran his fingers over the ancient cursive, faded now in its brown ink. The bishop wrote frustratingly in generalities rather than specifics, as most of his generation did, leaving many tantalizing questions unanswered, many problems unaddressed. Sam was never mentioned in the journal, but several familiar names jumped at him from the pages: Heber Golby, Jack Harper, Jim Peavey, Sister Treadwell, Billy Jones, and, of course, Eleanor Sullivan and her children. Lester Hawkins was there with Josiah Pratt.

Chadester wrote often of the Williams family and little Joey. In a sweet but minor detail, he mentioned a "belt of blue and purple beads the young lad gave to Annabelle Sullivan at Christmas." He talked about being called to bless the boy before he died and how he broke his ankle getting through the storm, leaving the father "to manage on his own with others in the house." He said very little about Laney in the journal, except that she was a fine young woman and a childhood friend of John's. This particular diary ended in May of 1916, and some final pages were missing, so there were few conclusions drawn. There was one oblique reference to Mick Sullivan "drowning in his sins" but nothing directly written about his death.

The murders of George Sullivan and Lester Hawkins were tender subjects for Rone Chadester, and he discussed them often. His journal mentioned how initial suspicion had fallen on Rawley Swisher. Chadester mourned over his mistakes. It was as if he had somehow shirked his duty because a killer had come into the flock and such a tragedy had happened on his watch. He grieved endlessly about it in his journal, questioning his actions, wondering if he had done enough for Eleanor Sullivan, and even for Mick, before and after his involvement was known. *Perhaps I could have saved poor Lester Hawkins*, he'd recorded, *had I been on my guard and closer to the whisperings of the Spirit.*

Chadester wrote about Detectives Miller and Crenshaw and the posse he and John had joined to help track Mick down. He mentioned Bob Chambers, the deputy who was wounded in the effort. Apparently, John did go back to the Butcher place for a wagon once Chambers was injured, and the mishap led to Sullivan's escape. Sam remembered how Bishop Rone had worried over that decision, praying that it didn't mean calamity for some unknown victim later on. He imagined with horror how Chadester must have scourged himself after Laney's death, although the journal ended before anything was written to reveal his feelings in that regard.

Mostly, the journal became a tangible link into another world for Sam. He read in it repeatedly, all the little mundane things that took him back to 1915 Alpine, the fields and the streets and the antique chapel and the mercantile store. He ran his fingers down its broken spine, knowing that Bishop Chadester had once handled it. He studied the name on the front, embossed in gold, and knew that John had undoubtedly seen it. He clasped it to his chest at night and said his prayers, thanking God that he had learned to know and love the people in this book.

But it was Laney, of course, who still owned all of his deepest thoughts. In his worst nightmares, he could still see her and hear her screaming as she went into the rushing water locked in Sullivan's arms. He could still see them as the roiling waves quickly spun them away and out of reach. He could still feel himself screaming Laney's name as he watched the river take her, only to wake up and find himself screaming at a hospital orderly instead. Laney was gone, but she was still part of him and always would be. The journal was important because it was a link to her.

One day while he was still at the hospital, he told David his story. He told him all about his visit to the past, about Laney and their romance, about his blessing of Joey, about John's sturdy example of friendship and sacrifice and service. He told him about the hike into the canyon and how much he cherished the girl Mick Sullivan took from him, how he had felt at last the depth of real love. David seemed the perfect person to confide in, to tell these things that no one else would believe. After all, didn't he spend his working days buried in the past? Wouldn't he, of all people, understand how real it could be?

David was a sympathetic listener, to be sure. He was pleased, in fact, that the journal had made a difference, had really helped Sam stay connected. He tried to take Sam seriously. He even tried to take away the sting of his obviously fantasized experience. "Maybe Laney survived the river," he said. "You don't know for certain that she drowned. Maybe she swam out."

"Her hands were tied," Sam said disgustedly, knowing that his brother was patronizing him.

"Look, Sam"—David shrugged—"whatever happened to you, I thank God for it. You're a changed guy. Really, you are. You seem to have learned something while you were asleep, something about life and love and work and all the rest of it. The doc says you're working like a trooper with those machines he's got you on. You'll be out of here in no time, and we can start over being a family again. I know Mom and Dad are looking forward to getting better acquainted with the new you."

Sam nodded. It was no use telling any of them anything. He began to think it *was* all a dream, prompted in his damaged brain by the words from David's book. But then he remembered Laney's kisses, the sweet smell of her hair, the curve of her cheek as they sat together in the moonlight. She had been as real to him as life itself.

Part of his rehabilitation involved projects that forced him to use and strengthen his fingers, and the drills progressed in intricacy as he proved capable. He was startled one day when he was presented with a kit containing all the materials needed for creating a beaded concho belt. He set to work with both eagerness and apprehension as the crooked blue-and-purple design that Joey Williams had conceived came alive again, both in his memory and in his hands.

"You're slightly off on some of the lines," said the therapist's assistant. "Follow the pattern perfectly next time, and we'll know you're just where you should be."

"Sometimes crooked is creative," Sam answered. "I knew a fella once who worked on that principle." He kept the belt, even though the therapist didn't consider it the best measure of his progress. He knew his motor skills were fine.

*   *   *

A while later, Sam's father faced him in a humble, awkward way. It was a side of Lee Carroll that Sam had never seen before. They were walking in the pines behind the house, clad in heavy jackets against a February chill. Mr. Carroll's hands were jammed in his pockets, and his breath was warm when he suddenly turned and looked at Sam straight on. "Your accident changed everything, you know." His voice cracked as he spoke. "I thought I hated you for how callow you'd become. Then you nearly died, and I realized I didn't give two hoots about your immaturity, flippancy, worldliness, and that sort of thing. I loved you and that's all that mattered. I loved you, and I never thought I'd have another chance to tell you just how much."

"You hated me?"

"Well"—his father flushed—"I was darned disappointed."

Sam slapped his father's shoulder. "Ah, Dad," he said, "we've got a lot of making up to do."

Sam embraced his father there in the cold. He was uncomfortable with the situation and not quite ready to trust this newfound intimacy, but an image of Moroni Chadester with John in the churchyard suddenly flashed into his mind. His own father had reached out to him. He would try from his end to prove worthy of the effort.

*   *   *

"Hey, Dad," he asked his father once soon after that, while musing about a long ago blue sky and a blistering summer afternoon, "have you ever baled hay or driven an old jalopy down a dusty road?"

"Sure I have. Your great-grandfather Hansen had a ranch in Brigham when I was a kid. I sat beside him on the baler lots of times. I drove his old Ford, too, when I got to be about fourteen. Every rural boy's done that."

"How come you never told me?"

"You're kind of a modern kid, Sam. You've never been that interested in old-time stuff, like hay balers and jalopies. In fact, before your accident, it was kind of hard to get you interested in anything except fast cars and those 'smart' toys you carry around."

Sam looked at the phone in his hand. He almost cried. "We've got to stay connected, Dad. This phone, with all its miracles, doesn't work unless it's connected to something greater than itself . . . like a network or a power source."

"Or a family?" Carroll smiled. "A father who loves you? The Church? The priesthood? God?" He put his arm across Sam's shoulder. "David's been telling me a little bit about Moroni Chadester's journal. I wish I'd been closer to you, the way Chadester was to his son. But it's not too late. I think we've both been given a second chance to find some common ground."

Sam nodded. "I'd like that." He could almost feel Bishop Rone tapping him on the shoulder.

* * *

As soon as Sam was released from the hospital, he began a data search of 1915–16 crime records in Utah County. David helped him, and together they found Mick Sullivan's name connected to a murder investigation, although there were no more than a few minor details. Mick was listed under Michael (Mick or Mickey) Sullivan, Alpine: Investigated for felony murder. Death by drowning, May 1916.

"That's him," he told David. "That's Moroni Chadester's Mick Sullivan."

"It'll be interesting to compare notes on this guy. We'll add this to our research."

"It also proves what I said about him going into the river. It says here he drowned."

"It doesn't mention a woman with him."

"Let's keep looking. This is his record, not hers."

They did look, in every database they could think of. Elaine Williams from Alpine was nowhere to be found.

"She was real, Davy," said Sam in exasperation. "I swear she was!"

David put his hand on his brother's shoulder. "I know she was real, Sam. At least, in your mind, at least for a while. She got you through this thing, don't you see? A beautiful girl who loved you. What guy wouldn't fight to stick around for that? And you learned a few things about love and friendship and maturity, just like you said." He held up Chadester's journal again. "You're welcome to research these folks all you want, little brother. I'm glad you woke up feeling a connection to them. But you need to realize that some of them were part of your imagination." He straightened up in his chair and added with some gravity, "And since what happened to Laney was kind of brutal, you probably should be glad the poor girl didn't really exist, don't you think? At least not exactly in the way you remember her."

This startled Sam. "I guess you're right," he conceded. "I hadn't really thought of it like that."

"Well, it's something to consider."

Sam backed away from his memories then, or at least he tried to. David was right, he told himself. He was healing. He was young. He was ready to live again. He had dodged a bullet on I-15. It was time to move on.

He'd gotten into the habit of taking the commuter train to Provo to see David. The doctors wouldn't let him drive yet, so the train had provided a relaxing, convenient way to make the journey. The problem was he could see Timpanogos from his window, rising snow-capped in the eastern sky. The cleft of American Fork Canyon looked just as it did to Moroni Chadester coming home from a fishing trip on Utah Lake.

Sam would stare at those scenes as the train took him to Provo, and once, on a whim, he got off at the American Fork stop and walked up First East to the old tabernacle on the corner. The traffic rushing by and the bustle at the market across the street was a far cry from the scene he remembered when he went with Laney to the Christmas concert so long ago. The building still said *Alpine* in large letters on the front of the façade, although Sam was certain this yellow brick-tabernacle hadn't been connected with Alpine Stake for years.

Months went by, and Sam began to recognize how his accident had changed him. Grateful for a second chance, he went back to school and took his classes seriously, especially those that dealt with history, in which he took a fresh and abiding interest. Surprising himself and his family, he became more emotionally invested in his neighborhood, even deciding to remain a member of his parents' ward for a while. He never failed to attend sacrament meeting, and he devoted himself to his home teaching families, some of whom had special needs. One teen-aged boy reminded him of Tommy Sullivan. His lower lip stuck out, and his eyes dared Sam to shake his hand. Sam's first impulse was to toss the kid through the nearest screen door. But he held back. John Chadester knew how to handle kids straight off; Sam would have to earn what some men were gifted with, but he was determined to try. The blessing he remembered giving Joey taught him that he had a special gift as well, if he remained worthy of it. It was real. It was good. It was his to use for the benefit of others, and in it lay the core of his own manhood, of what God wanted him to be. Life was good.

Still, he could not forget.

When Sam was cleared to drive, he thought about going to Alpine just to look the place over and see if there was anything he recognized. It was summer, and there was a short break before fall semester. The view would be beautiful, he knew, even if modern homes now dotted all the foothills and the benches where John and Laney used to ride. He hesitated, however, feeling perhaps that his memories in the dark were better left undisturbed. The reality of modern times in Alpine might be a jolt to his sensibilities, he chuckled to himself. A wonderful dream should stay a dream, lest its illusions be shattered. So each time he passed the Alpine exit on his way to Provo, he slowed but, in the end, drove by.

The day he finally stopped was in September, and he only took the off-ramp because David had badgered him into running down the pioneer journal of a man whose family lived in Highland.

"Apparently, this fellow crossed the plains in 1867," David said. "That makes his journal pure gold to a historian, if it's authentic. Just see what kind of shape it's in, and let me know."

When Sam realized that Highland and Alpine were on the same exit ramp, he felt a slight twist in his heart, and he found himself lingering with the Highland family so long that they invited him to stay for dinner. He politely declined, praising the great-great grandfather's dusty diary even further, and when he finally backed out the door, he dreaded what he knew could not be put off any longer.

Slowly, he drove to Alpine, a lovely country enclave now, filled with expensive homes and shops and professional suites and village malls. The town's pioneer heritage had not been forgotten. There were museums, art centers, and parks anchored by commemorative statues and monuments. Some of the old brick homes were still there. Sam even recognized two or three from the 1915 era. But the streets were wide and paved, the cars raced by, and the little antique church with the secret hideaway under its steeple was gone. Nothing really looked the same.

But there was one place Sam knew his friends would be. It was the place he'd dreaded seeing all along. Facing his vivid memories one last time, he made his way to the cemetery on the hill, with no doubt that he could walk straight to Joey Williams's grave, where he had stood, head bowed in grief, with Laney and Kit and Johanna on that awful winter day. He knew George Sullivan and Lester Hawkins were nearby too, for he'd seen them laid to rest and remembered the area well. And now, how many others would there be?

Almost before he was ready to begin the pilgrimage, there he was. He parked his car and made his way under the trees to the paved cemetery path, trembling as he took in the old graveyard, beautifully kept and cared for, still guarded by the towering mountains he had come to love. He found Joey first, because even though the place had swelled in size, he knew right where to go. The wooden cross was gone, replaced by a headstone that included the names of Kenneth "Kit" and Johanna but not Laney. Sam frowned at this. He was suddenly jolted by the notion that they might never have found Laney's body, and pain seared through him, as he thought of their sorrow rather than his own. In all his ache for Laney, all his personal horror at losing her, he had never given much thought to what it must have meant to Kit and Johanna, their only remaining child. The one thing they both lived to treasure. He knelt a long time before that family's stone and prayed that they had been reunited in the afterlife and that the blessing he had pronounced on Joey had come true, that he was somewhere walking tall. A joyous warmth flooded through him, and he knew it was true.

Next, he found the Chadesters, Moroni and Margaret. He noticed that the bishop had lived until 1940 and his wife until 1949. His own grandparents could have known them and would have been alive at the same time, although younger. The generations overlapped, David had reminded him. "We miss so many wonderful people each time the world switches over."

There were several family members buried around the Chadester parents, including Andrew and his wife and children, but Sam didn't see

John's name right away. He turned back to Bishop Rone's marker and contemplated again what a fine father this man had been, to both his son and his community. "Dear Bishop Rone," Sam whispered, "there's not enough room on any stone to list all the good you did."

Sam finally rose from the Chadester grave and made one more effort to find John. "Come on, bud, where are you?" he pleaded aloud. "Did you get killed in some war somewhere? Are you buried in some far-off Flanders Field after giving your all for God and country? That sounds like something you'd do. World War I came along in your time, didn't it? I'll bet you went off over there with the Dough Boys and became a hero and never came home to good old Alpine again. Is that what happened?"

Suddenly, Sam saw a smooth, gray slab, simple yet majestic in its grace. It stood before him like a bulletin from heaven, and as the words melted into his soul, he had to blink to absorb the shock. There were two names on the stone, a married couple buried side by side after a long life together, as witnessed by the dates engraved before him.

Chadester

John Benjamin   Elaine Williams
1893–1975   1894–1970
Married June 29, 1917

"Laney! Laney!" Sam gasped and threw his arms in the air. He jumped three feet off the ground. People visiting nearby graves looked up in dismay at such rude behavior in a cemetery. Sam didn't even see them. "Laney! You made it! Somehow, some way, you made it! That no-good rat Sullivan drowned, but *you* made it!"

Sam fell to his knees in front of the headstone. He felt it with his hands and ran his fingers over the letters. He read the names and the dates over and over again. "John, you old scalawag, you got the girl after all! I can't believe it! Yes I can. Yes I can. It was meant to be, old friend. All those years. It was meant to be!" Sam took hold of the headstone on both sides and bowed his head against the face of it. "Oh, Laney," he murmured, "Laney, Laney, Laney . . . I'm glad you lived . . . even without me."

I think she's destiny's child, Sam, and meant in the end for just one man. I'll be pleased to see that destiny come to pass . . .

* * *

Sam visited the Alpine graveyard frequently after that. He learned from the other names there that John and Laney had five children. It interested him that one of the boys was named Samuel, although Biblical names seemed to be favored all around. He never told anyone in Alpine who he was or why he came so often. His connection with these people was a private joy that he didn't particularly want to share. He didn't mention it to David either. It was like not wanting to share a favorite book or movie with someone for fear they wouldn't be as enthusiastic as you'd hoped. Sharing wasn't worth risking the disappointment.

"You're crazy, man, to keep thinking about all of this," he would often tell himself. And sometimes he would purposely try to let life get in the way. He occupied himself with school, he got a job doing data work for David. He even made a real effort not to visit Alpine quite as much. He decided this was for the best. He was making progress; he knew he needed to move on.

But in the end, it was no use. Something haunted him. Something kept drawing him back—images that wouldn't leave his mind, echoes that would never quite be silent.

One night he was looking at the blue-and-purple concho belt, the one he had made as part of his therapy, thinking of Joey.

"I'm going to take this down to Alpine," he told his mother. "There's a grave there I want to decorate."

"Alpine?" said his mother. "Who do we know in Alpine?"

"David introduced me to some people there."

His mother took the beaded belt and scrutinized it. "You've certainly improved since you made this," she said, patting his cheek. "I want to cry when I look at it."

"So do I."

Chapter Fifteen

THIS TRIP TO ALPINE CAME on a bright spring day. The cemetery was green again after another dreary winter, and the mountain peaks were just beginning to lose their frosty mantle. Sam visited Joey's grave, as was his custom, then the Chadesters, and finished up by kneeling at the headstone of John and Laney.

He'd intended to leave the concho belt with Joey, but since he thought this might be his last time, he saved it for this final grave. Some people had parked their car on the road a ways down, and two women sat by one of the monuments as their children played under the trees. Sam had hoped to be alone on this last visit, but the visitors were far enough away and didn't really bother him. There were others in the group, as well, but their attention seemed to be directed at the lower section, and Sam soon forgot about them too. He had one thing on his mind.

He spoke aloud to John and Laney, as he always did. "Hey, John, did you ever get another Saxon? I'll bet you kicked yourself in 1960 when you found out how much that thing was worth by then.

"Hey, Laney, what's the idea marrying this guy? You were my girl, don't you remember? I got a concho belt here that reminds me of Joey. 'Crooked sometimes means creative.' Right?

"Laney, how'd you ever get away from ol' Mick Sullivan? How'd you ever swim those rapids with your hands tied, huh? Did you have an angel on your shoulder I never knew about? I'll find out some day. I swear I will."

So caught up was Sam in his fantasies that he didn't hear the young woman approach until she was right next to him. When she spoke he had to turn and squint, for the sun was just behind her. "Hello," she said. "I'm wondering how you know these people. You've been up here a long time, and I could swear, you seem to be talking to them!"

Sam shaded his eyes and couldn't believe what he was seeing. Tongue-tied, he slowly rose to his feet and tried to keep from falling over. "I . . . I think I used to know the couple buried here," he finally managed to stutter. "I'm not from Alpine, so I'm not really sure."

"Well, I can tell you who they are," replied the girl, who looked college age and swayed her honey-colored hair. "They're my great-great grandparents, John and Laney Chadester. Everyone in Alpine knows this grave, but I don't know you. So when I saw you here, I had to come and find out who you were."

"You called her Laney," said Sam, amazed.

"Everybody did," replied the girl. "*Elaine* is what you put on birth certificates and tombstones, Mama always says. My name's Laney too. I'm named for her, as you can probably guess."

"Did . . . did you know her?"

"Oh, no. I'm only twenty-three. Grandma died years before my mother was even born. But that doesn't mean we don't remember her—and Grandpa too. They were quite the pair, I guess."

"You look like her," said Sam, almost without thinking. This Laney's eyes were so blue he was immediately lost in them. "It's uncanny how much you look like her."

"Now, how would you know that?" The girl smiled.

"I just know."

"You still haven't told me who you are. And what's that Indian belt you have? It looks familiar."

Sam looked down at the concho belt and, on an impulse, gave it to her.

She turned it over in her hands, seeming fascinated with its pattern. She moved to a nearby granite bench and sat with it in her lap, studying it further, while Sam made a point of studying her. Her resemblance to the girl he knew was incredible. It was as if his Laney had been transported to the present day, put in skinny jeans, and dropped right down next to him at the Alpine Cemetery.

"We have one like this at home," said the new Laney, still fingering the belt. "It's a hundred years old or something like that. It's come down through the family. It's one of my mom's most prized possessions. She says it was made by Grandma Laney's brother not long before he died. It's all old and threadbare, and a lot of the beads are gone, but I swear it looks a lot like this. Same colors anyway."

The two of them looked at each other, both silent for a moment. The sun was setting behind them in the west, over those same hills where Miller's posse once tracked Mick Sullivan on a day like this one so long ago. The mountains above Alpine peered down as they had on Laney and her family that very afternoon.

"I still don't know your name," she finally said.

"It's Sam. Sam Carroll."

From the section below where the car was parked, someone called, "Laney, we're ready to leave."

"I'll be right there," the girl called back. She looked a long moment at Sam. "You know, you might want to come over and compare your concho belt with ours, since you seem to know so much about my great-great-grandmother."

"I'd like that."

"It would be pretty cool if the belts turned out to be alike or even kinda close."

The belts . . . and other things as well.

"Very cool," he said.

Later, after they had exchanged addresses and phone numbers, the honey-haired girl departed with her family. Sam sat beside the grave again and considered the lessons of eternity. He was in a trance. He couldn't move. For the rest of the afternoon, he sat there by that headstone, and when the stars came out, he lay on his back and looked up at them. A caretaker came by and nudged him, or he may have stayed all night. His last words were to the stars and to John Chadester's name in front of him. "Maybe it was all because of the journal. I don't know, Johnny. Maybe I was never really there at all, but for everything that happened and everything I learned, I'm gonna go on thinking I was. I'll be glad until the day I die that for a little while, your problems were my problems, your joys my joys, and your time in this world was my time too."

* * *

"Sammy's certainly a changed man since his recovery," said David's wife, Trish, to her mother-in-law at a family barbeque that summer. "He seems so much more focused and connected to the things that matter. I think he really appreciates how blessed he is, and he's making the most of having a second chance at life."

"It might be that new girlfriend of his in Alpine," said Dorothy Carroll happily. "She's a gem, you know."

David, sitting near them, listened as he watched his brother play with Gwen and Robbie on the grass by their backyard trampoline.

"What do you think, Dave?" said Trish. "Is it love that's changing Sammy?"

"Yeah, I think it is," mused David. "That and a very old book I read to him while he was fast asleep."

About the Author

LYNNE LARSON IS A MUCH-PUBLISHED author of stories and articles related to religion, history, and literature. The pioneer Church, and especially its women, is a theme of special interest. A retired teacher, she devotes her time to promoting education in the humanities, as well as a love of Western history, at every opportunity. She is a graduate of Brigham Young University and holds a master's degree in English from Idaho State University in Pocatello. She and her husband, Kent, are the parents of three grown children.